**HICCUP HORRENDOUS HADDOCK
THE THIRD HAS ACCIDENTALLY
FOUND HIMSELF HAVING TO
COMPLETE THE IMPOSSIBLE TASK.**

Whilst searching for his lost friend
Camicazi, Hiccup and the Hooligan Tribe have
ended up on Uglithug Island. Now **UG**, the most
brutal King in the World, thinks Hiccup **LOVES**
his daughter. Hiccup must venture to the
Isle of Berserk to pass his test or **DIE** trying. Gulp.

Oh and guess who is back? Only Hiccup's
DREADED arch-enemy, Alvin the Treacherous,
who is seeking revenge . . .

Can Hiccup find Camicazi, succeed in
his task and escape Alvin – **AGAIN?**

You don't **HAVE** to read the Hiccup books in order.
But if you want to, this is the right order:

1. How to train your Dragon
2. How to be a Pirate
3. How to speak Dragonese
4. How to Cheat a Dragon's Curse
5. How to Twist a Dragon's Tale
6. A Hero's Guide to Deadly Dragons
7. How to Ride a Dragon's Storm
8. How to Break a Dragon's Heart
9. How to Steal a Dragon's Sword
10. How to Seize a Dragon's Jewel
11. How to Betray a Dragon's Hero
12. How to Fight a Dragon's Fury

JOIN HICCUP ON HIS QUEST
(although he doesn't quite realise he is on one yet...)

THE PROPHECY OF
THE KING'S LOST THINGS

'The Dragontime is coming
And only a King can save you now.
The King shall be the
Champion of Champions.

You shall know the King
By the King's Lost Things.
A fang-free dragon, my second-best sword,
My Roman shield,
An arrow-from-the-land-that-does-not-exist,
The heart's stone, the key-that-opens-all-locks,
The ticking-thing, the Throne, the Crown.

And last and best of all the ten,
The Dragon Jewel shall save all men.'

Hiccup
Horrendous
Haddock III

TOOTHLESS
Hiccup's
highly
disobedient
hunting
dragon

FISHLEGS
Hiccup's best friend

GOBBER
THE
BELCH

Teacher in charge of
the Pirate Training
Programme on Berk

DOGSBREATH
the DUHBRAIN
Snotlout's friend and
fellow bully.

Camicazi
Heir to
the Bog-Burglar
Tribe

Snotlout wants to be the next Chief of the Hooligan Tribe

Snotface Snotlout (Hiccup's cousin)

THE CHIEF BERSERK

(likes feeding people to the Beast in wicker basket i.e. mad as a banana

Stoick the Vast
Tough but slightly dim Chief of the Hooligan Tribe
(Hiccup's father)

I dedicate this book to my parents, Michael and Marcia,

HODDER CHILDREN'S BOOKS

First published in Great Britain in 2009 by Hodder & Stoughton
This edition published in 2017 by Hodder & Stoughton

5 7 9 10 8 6 4

SPECIAL EDITION

Text and illustrations copyright © 2009 Cressida Cowell

The moral rights of the author have been asserted.

A CIP catalogue record for this book is available from the British Library.

ISBN: 978-1-444-93983-5

Cover design by Jennifer Stephenson
Background cover illustration by Christopher Gibbs

Printed and bound by Clays Ltd, St Ives plc

The paper and board used in this book are made from wood from responsible sources.

MIX
From responsible sources
FSC® C104740
FSC
www.fsc.org

Hodder Children's Books
An imprint of Hachette Children's Group, Part of Hodder & Stoughton
Carmelite House, 50 Victoria Embankment, London EC4Y 0DZ
An Hachette UK Company
www.hachette.co.uk

"The past haunts the present in more ways than we think. It certainly scares the living daylights out of ME."

Old Wrinkly

How to Break a Dragon's Heart

written and illustrated by

CRESSIDA COWELL

Hodder
Children's
Books

A division of Hachette Children's Group

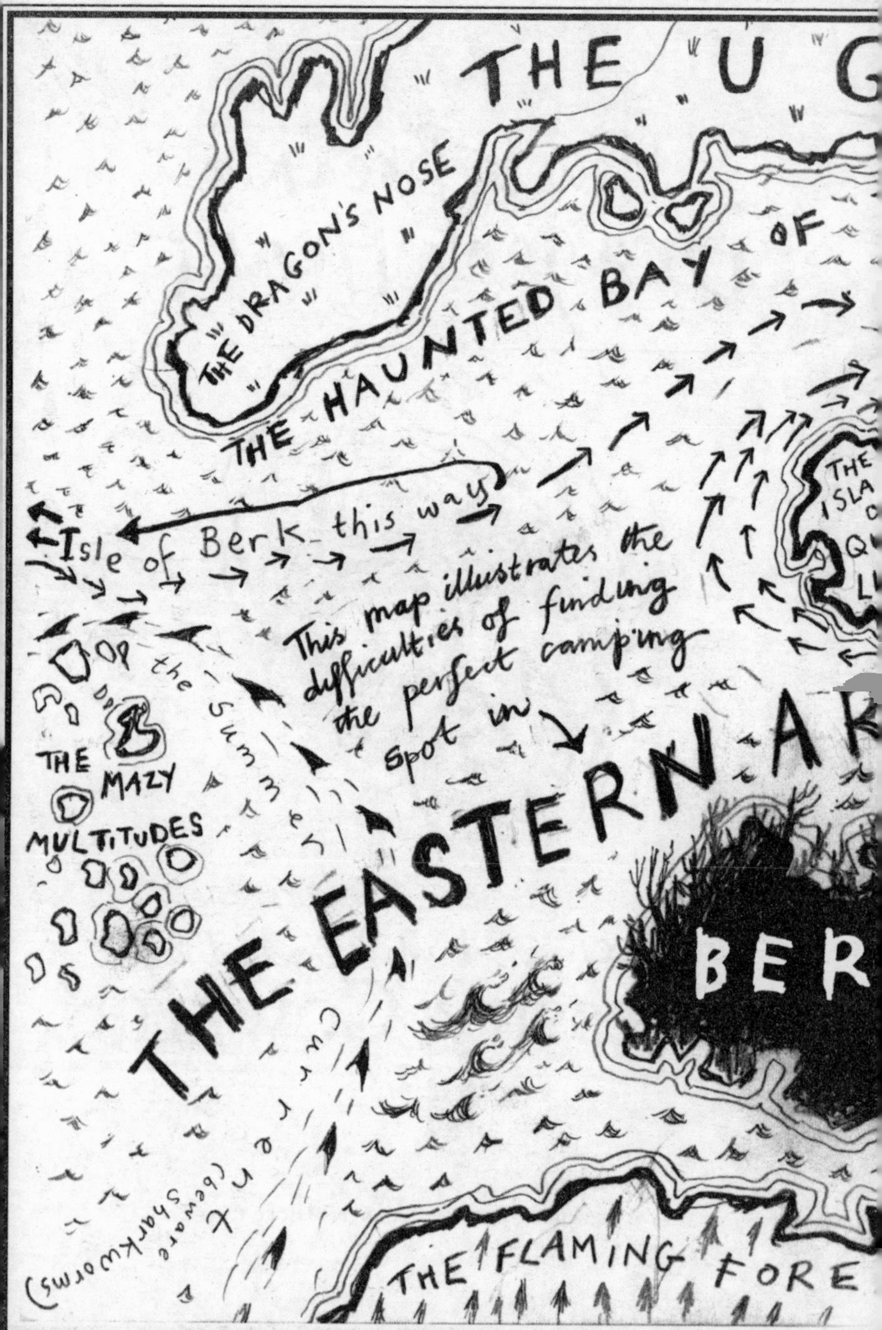

THE "U G

THE DRAGON'S NOSE

THE HAUNTED BAY OF

Isle of Berk this way

This map illustrates the difficulties of finding the perfect camping spot in

THE EASTERN AR

THE
ISLA
O
Q
LI

of the Summe

THE
MAZY
MULTITUDES

BER

(beware Sharkworms)

THE FLAMING FORE

In the summer of 2002, a boy digging on a beach found a box that contained the following papers.

They are the eighth volume of memoirs of Hiccup Horrendous Haddock the Third, the famous Viking Hero, Dragon-whisperer and Top Swordfighter.

They tell the story of how he faced the dreadful fate of being fed to the Beast in a wicker basket on the island of Berserk, and how he found out the secret of the Lost Throne of the Wilderwest, and what happened to his ancestor, Hiccup Horrendous Haddock the Second...

~ CONTENTS ~

Hiccup Horrendous
Haddock the Third
and his sword,
the 'Endeavour'

PROLOGUE BY HICCUP HORRENDOUS HADDOCK III THE LAST OF THE GREAT VIKING HEROES

History is a ghost story.

My own childhood has passed into history, and the ghosts I find there are the ghosts of Heroes, and Dragons, and Berserks and witches, and it has became fashionable not to believe in these things any more.

But I believe, for I was there.

And just because YOU, dear Reader, have never seen a dragon or a witch, or a ghost, does not necessarily mean that they do not exist.

This Quest is the story of the most important moment in my entire life so far.

It was the first time I learnt that the names on the flat map of the Archipelago, such as the Bay of the Broken Heart, were not just made-up fantastical names, but names that related to real people who had real, flesh and blood lives and the things that happened to them still haunted the place where I was growing up.

That is what *I* mean by ghosts.

The Lost Throne of the Wilderwest

Peering above the great grey remorseless ocean,
Poking defiantly out of the endless, ever-changing sea,
Is the broken back of an island like a humpback whale,
And somewhere in the wind-tossed, storm-blown grasses
Where the wind howls across the blasted heather
And the trees are all blown into hoops,
Are the two stout stone stumps on which once stood
The Everlasting Throne of the Kings of the Wilderwest.

HERE sat Grimbeard the Ghastly, the Last Great King,
Looking out over the rooftops of his bustling Viking city,
Stroking his great sword, the Stormblade.
And HERE where the seagulls circle
And the wolves gather pace
For the hunt across the marshes
Was once a harbour for a hundred ships
That Grimbeard sent to the north, south, east, and west,
Seizing plunder, treasure and slaves, in jolly Viking fashion.

HERE he once stood, clenched his fist, and shouted:
'I NAME THIS LAND TOMORROW FOR IT SHALL
LAST FOR EVERMORE!'
And a thousand men lifted up their spears
And shouted their approval,
While the dragons winked their ancient eyes as if to say,
'We have heard all this before...'

HERE he was betrayed by his own flesh and blood
In the middle of a game of chess…
HERE is where he spilt that blood,
The blood of his own son, on the kingly marble…
HERE the flames licked the sky as the city went up
Like a million candles…
HERE the bright clean sound of sword on sword…
HERE the harbour crammed berry-red with corpses…
And HERE, the defeated Warrior-King looked back
To see several lifetimes' worth of dreams go up in smoke
As his boat began to limp like a wounded wolf
Across the sea to the Island of Despair.

And that was the end of the Last King of the Wilderwest.
The Throne was lost, the chess pieces scattered
Across the ocean, the Stormblade buried,
The Kingdom shattered
Into a hundred warring Tribes again.
And Grimbeard sailed into the west
Never to be seen again.

But HERE was where it once all happened.
HERE where the eagles soar
Over knotted rags of brambles.
And the sea-filled caves in the bleak black cliffs echo
To the ache of no human voice.

MIDSUMMER STORM

There are many storms in the Barbaric Archipelago.

But *this* was the greatest storm in over one hundred years.

It came, without warning, at the height of midsummer.

For three days it raged without stopping, howling like a god in pain, blowing over houses, tearing up trees, picking up ships and tossing them down into the depths of the ocean as if they were matches, caring nothing for the tiny human habitations clinging like ants to the barren island wildernesses, mowing them down as if they were nothing.

A storm like this causes many things to be lost, and many things to be found.

Many a boat can be dragged down in the tempest. And many a strange object that everyone had forgotten about can be dragged up from the depths of the ocean and tossed up on one of the beaches along with a whole heap of driftwood.

This particular Storm caused someone to be lost.

Camicazi, the tiny, intrepid, tangle-haired daughter of Big-Boobied Bertha, Chief of the Bog-Burglars, was out on the sea, alone in her boat

The Stormy Petrel,* when the storm struck.

Even before the tempest was past, the Bog-Burglars were out looking for her. And when the winds finally dropped and the Tribes of the Archipelago were waking up to the devastation of flattened cowsheds and walls and houses and upside-down trees, and were wearily getting down to the task of rebuilding their lives again, the Bog-Burglars were already scouring the very edges of the Archipelago in their black-sailed boats, shouting:

'Caaa-aaaa-m-a-c-aaaaaaaaaaaaziiiiiiiiiiiiii!'
'Caaa-aaaa-m-a-c-aaaaaaaaaaaaziiiiiiiiiiiiii!'
'Caaa-aaaa-m-a-c-aaaaaaaaaaaaziiiiiiiiiiiiii!'

But answer came there none.

* The Stormy Petrel is the smallest of the sea-birds. They were so named because sailors thought they warned of incoming storms.

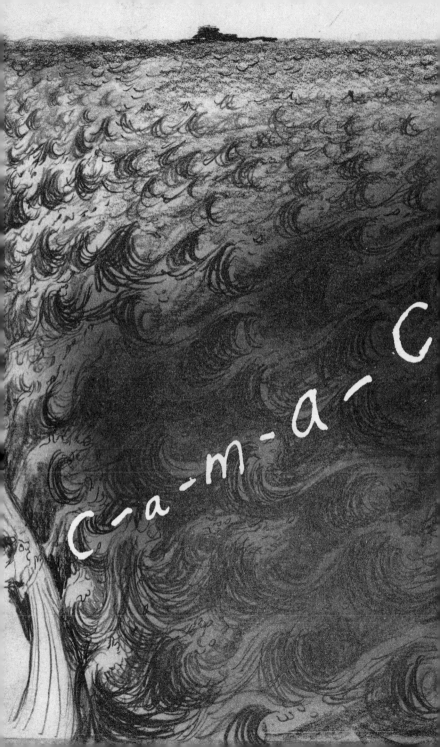

1. THE LOST CHILD

And so it was that one summer evening, two Hooligan ships were going round and round in circles around the little island of the Quiet Life in the Eastern Archipelago.

It was odd for Hooligan ships to be in the Eastern Archipelago, for that part of the world is exceptionally dangerous, and the Vikings tended to avoid it at all costs.

There are many many horrors in the Eastern Archipelago. The only reason the Hooligans were there at all was because they were helping Big-Boobied Bertha search for her missing daughter. And now evening was drawing in, and in their quest to find the lost child they had travelled far, far, far from their safe cosy little home on the Isle of Berk, and it was too late to go home.

They would have to drop anchor and spend the night in the Eastern Archipelago, never a happy thought. But where could they camp?

All the lands to the north and east were part of **UGLITHUG** territory, and the Uglithugs were slavers, and the wickedest pirates in the Barbaric World, and they had a tendency to kill any uninvited visitors on the spot. Besides, a lot of their beaches were haunted.

Of course, there was the island of Berserk.

But then again, the Berserkers went crazy on a full moon and howled like dogs and fed people in baskets to some nameless thing that lived in the wildness of the wood...

So that left the island of the Quiet Life as the *only* safe place in the Eastern Archipelago to spend the night.

Which was why the Hooligans had spent the last hour and a half going round and round it in circles, searching for the Perfect Camping Spot.

'HALT!' shouted Stoick the Vast, O Hear His Name and Tremble, Ugh, Ugh, the Chief of the Hairy Hooligan Tribe. He was an impressive figure with a magnificent red beard like a lion's mane that had been vigorously back-combed by maniacs.

'REST YOUR OARS A MOMENT!'

Stoick turned to his son, Hiccup Horrendous Haddock the Third, who was standing beside him on the deck of *The Fat Penguin*, peering anxiously over the figure-head, shielding his eyes from the setting sun as he scanned the horizon.

Hiccup was a most unlikely Heir to the Hooligan Tribe. An ordinary looking boy, with red hair, and long skinny limbs, and the kind of anxious freckled face that was easy to overlook in a crowd.

'Now, Hiccup,' said Stoick importantly. 'I want you to watch what I do carefully here. A Chief has to be ABSOLUTELY SURE that he finds a safe spot to camp. The wellbeing of his *entire Tribe* depends on him finding the PERFECT camping spot.'

'Yes, but we've been looking for ages now,' Hiccup pointed out. 'And there was a place back there on the island of the Quiet Life that looked really quite nice.'

'Too exposed,' pronounced Stoick gravely. 'The perfect spot should be sheltered from wind and sudden storms.'

'Yes, but Father, we're all quite tired and it's getting dark and the Eastern Archipelago is very

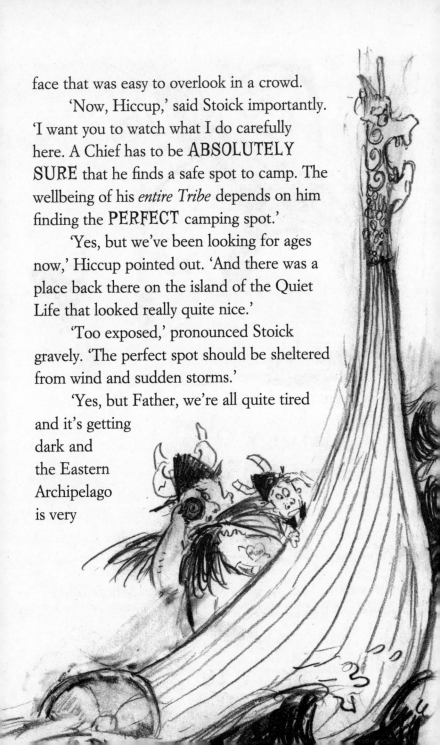

Watch and learn,
my boy. Watch
and learn.
Said Stoick.

dangerous,' Hiccup said. 'What about all those other places we looked at?'

'Too muddy, too many jellyfish, not enough

places to pitch the tents, no lookout area…' said
Stoick. 'You need to look for the PERFECT spot,
Hiccup.' He patted Hiccup condescendingly on the
back. 'That's why *I'm* the Captain, son. Watch and
learn, my boy, watch and learn.'

Stoick stalked off enthusiastically to look for
other suitable spots, while his crew rested their weary
arms and grumbled mutinously. Somebody said that
perhaps if Stoick was so keen to find the perfect
camping spot he might like to take
over at the oars.

But they said it very quietly, so
that Stoick wouldn't hear.

'I hate camping,' said Fishlegs,
Hiccup's best friend. 'It does terrible
things to my asthma.' Fishlegs was
a tall, spindly runner-bean of a boy,
who had eczema as well as asthma,
and was allergic to wheat and dairy.
Not to mention dragons.

'This is all *your* fault, Useless*…'
snarled Snotlout, Hiccup's cousin. Snotlout was a large
arrogant adolescent with a natural air of leadership and
a lot of skeleton tattoos. He spat thoughtfully into
the sea.

---

* Hiccup the Useless was Snotlout's nickname for Hiccup.

'We wouldn't be out here looking for a lousy little Bog-Burglar, if *you* hadn't turned your father soft, so that he made allies with those mud-trotting female no-hopers,' sneered Snotlout. 'Before you started interfering, there was an excellent saying, "the only good Bog-Burglar is a dead Bog-Burglar". And what I say is, if we find her dear ickle Bog-Burglar corpse floating down that gorge over there tomorrow morning, I, for one, will not be blubbing into my cocoa.'

'Har har har,' snorted Dogsbreath the Duhbrain, Snotlout's friend and fellow bully.

'You're such a charmer, Snotlout,' snapped Hiccup. 'No wonder you make friends easily.'

r-e-e-e-e-e-eac

'But seriously,' drawled Snotlout, 'look around you, Useless. You and your father have really put us in danger here. We've drifted into UGLITHUG territory. See that island over there?' Snotlout pointed to an ominous, brooding dark shape to the south, from which a strange, humming, drumming noise seemed to be coming. 'You want to know what *that* is, sweet-pea? That's BERSERK, that is. And *this* beach that we're drifting into now? This is the Beach of the Broken Heart...'

Dogsbreath the Duhbrain stopped giggling abruptly, and turned an unattractive shade of green. 'The Beach of the Broken Heart?' he stammered. 'But isn't that... supposed to be... *haunted*????'

'Sure is,' grinned Snotlout.

'*Haunted*????' squeaked Fishlegs.

Snotlout opened his eyes wide and leaned forward to Fishlegs,

out with her horrible ghosty fingers

whispering conspiratorially. 'That's right, you weed. The Beach of the Broken Heart is haunted, so they say, by a ghost-lady in a ghost-ship... searching for ever for her lost, dead child... and if she finds YOU instead... why' – and he paused, for effect – 'she reaches into your chest with her horrible ghosty fingers...' – Fishlegs and Dogsbreath both covered their chests hurriedly – '... and she takes out your beating heart and sails with it back to the ghost-world,' finished Snotlout with relish.

Dogsbreath was so anxious that he dropped his drawn dagger rather painfully on to his toe. 'OOOOW...'

'That is such RUBBISH, Snotlout,' said Hiccup loudly. 'That's just a myth, created because the marshes behind the beach are home to a rare kind of bird called the Neverbird, and it makes a sound like a crying ghost.'

Snotlout leant back and crossed his tattooed arms casually. '*Is* it rubbish though?' he said. 'We could be in serious danger here. And all for a dirty little Bog-Burglar who has nothing to do with the Hooligan Tribe. I repeat. All *your* fault, Useless.'

And it was just at that moment that Hiccup's hunting-dragon Toothless returned to *The Fat Penguin*

Toothless, Hiccup's dragon, being VERY BUSY and IMPORTANT

from
a scouting
mission, making a
clumsy crash-landing on
Hiccup's head.

Hiccup had sent Toothless ahead to investigate coves and rocks and beaches and likely places where a small boat might have been blown and wrecked by a mighty storm.

If Hiccup was an unlikely Heir to the Hooligan Tribe, Toothless was an even more unlikely hunting-dragon-to-the-Heir. He was a Common-or-Garden dragon, the least rare of the dragon species (although he claimed to be something much more exotic), and he was at least half the size of the other young Warriors' hunting-dragons. He had no obvious weapons and, as his name suggests, no teeth.

At the moment he was genuinely anxious, but the drama of the search, and the lateness of the hour, and the importance of *him*, Toothless, leading the hunt from the front, not to mention the fact that he had missed two meals and two naps, had led him to cross the line into hopeless, fidgety, over-excitement.

He was wound up tighter than a tick who had feasted on several, large, sugar-laced cups of coffee.

Toothless always had a stammer, but now he was so beside himself he couldn't even get the words out. He just jumped up and down on Hiccup's head, pointing his wings at the Beach of the Broken Heart.

'What is it, Toothless? What is it?' asked Hiccup.* Stoick, who was squinting all around him, and discussing with his second-in-command the relative merits of different camping areas, spotted Toothless pointing, and turned his telescope towards the Beach of the Broken Heart.

'Well *that's* not a suitable camping spot,' Stoick grunted but then he stopped. 'Hang on a second. What's that? THERE'S SOMETHING ON THE BEACH OVER THERE!'

Could this be a Viking Telescope?

eyepiece ↙ under here

---

* Hiccup was one of the few Vikings before, or since, who was able to speak Dragonese, the language the dragons spoke to each other.

2. THE SOMETHING ON THE BEACH

Poor Fishlegs jumped two
feet in the air, thinking that
the Something might be
a ghost-lady.

But it was
Something large
and solid sticking
up out of the
white sands of the
Beach of the Broken Heart.

'Maybe it's Camicazi's boat!' cried Hiccup
hopefully, screwing up his eyes and trying to see.
'Perhaps it crashed and it's sticking kind of upwards
out of the sand...'

'WARRIORS!' bellowed Stoick. 'LET US
INVESTIGATE THE SOMETHING ON THE
BEACH BEFORE WE CARRY ON LOOKING FOR
THE PERFECT CAMPING SPOT! IT COULD BE
THE MISSING CHILD WE'VE BEEN LOOKING
FOR!'

The Warriors were a little reluctant, to say
the least.

The sun was sinking rapidly, in a beautiful display of pink and red and gold. However, no one was in the mood to appreciate a lovely sunset. Was it their imaginations, or was that drumming noise coming from the direction of the island of Berserk getting louder?

'But Chief,' Nobber Nobrains pointed out, 'that beach over there is not only *haunted*, it is also part of the territory of UG the Uglithug.'

UG the Uglithug didn't like visitors.

'Well we're not going to *land* or anything are we?' barked Stoick the Vast. 'We're just going to check it out... and what are you doing questioning my orders? I AM THE CAPTAIN OF THIS SHIP AND YOU SHOULD OBEY WITHOUT QUESTION!'

So they oared their weary way towards the Something on the beach, grumbling as they went.

'O Useless, you're such a delight, I could just smack your Useless fat head,' snarled Snotlout savagely. 'And I *would* if I wasn't too tired and hungry to be bothered.'

But as they drew nearer, into the shallower water of the Bay, through a jigsaw of floating driftwood that had been thrown up by the storm, even in the failing light of the dying evening it clearly wasn't a boat.

'It's too rectangular,' said Fishlegs.

What could it be?

Fishlegs had just decided in his head that it was a COFFIN when there was a sudden CRRRUNCCH!! from the ship's bottom and they came to an abrupt halt.

'FOOLS!' yelled Stoick. 'You've hit a rock!'

'You didn't tell us to stop,' pointed out Nobber Nobrains, not unreasonably. '*You're* the Captain. *We* just obey orders.'

They had hit a rock, and holed the boat.

Water poured in from the starboard side.

And *The Fat Penguin* gently laid her very fat bottom on the sand of the Beach of the Broken Heart and refused to move.

It is always embarrassing for a Viking when he sinks his own boat.

Especially in only two feet of water.

It *is* an occupational hazard.

THUNDERING Thighs and GINGERY WHISKERS AND LITTLE TWIRLY BITS OF THE GREAT GOD THOR !!!

But it could not have happened at a more awkward time.

The Vikings got out of the boat. The water was knee-deep. Tactfully, nobody said anything.

'THUNDERING THIGHS AND GINGERY WHISKERS AND LITTLE TWIRLY BITS OF THE GREAT GOD THOR!' exclaimed Stoick the Vast, bright red in the face. As he shook his fist at the heavens above, the last blink of sun disappeared on the horizon, and there they were, stranded on the

36

Beach of the Broken Heart until they could mend the boat in the morning.

'RIGHT!' shouted Stoick the Vast. 'I think we've found our camp for the night.'

The Hooligans on the other boat weren't so very keen to join them on the beach. '*Our* boat is all right,' called out Baggybum the Beerbelly. 'We might just stay aboard and sleep here…'

'WHADDAYATALKING ABOUT?' roared Stoick the Vast. 'HOOLIGANS STAND TOGETHER! GET OUT HERE DOUBLE QUICK!'

It was not what you might call the *perfect* camping spot. But what choice did they have?

The sun had sunk.

So had their boat.

The moon was coming up, and the first of the Glow-worms were beginning to light up the still evening air.

Too tired to argue, the Hooligans anchored the other boat where it was, and threw their animal skin blankets over their shoulders, and waded through the knee-high water and up and on to the beach.

At least they found out what the Something on the beach was.

It was a Throne.

37

An enormous, empty THRONE.

It was carved out of a single piece of white
marble, but it had obviously just come out of the
water, for it was covered with a film of green algae,
and it was plastered as thickly with barnacles as if they
were jewels, and long trails of seaweed drifted from
the shell-encrusted arms.

The Throne was enormous, and such was
its solid position on the beach it was as if it were
inhabited by a giant invisible god, sitting there quietly,
looking out to sea.

'How extraordinary,' breathed Stoick the Vast.
'Where do you think *this* came from? *And the Hooligan
coat of arms is on the back!* This must belong to US...
How *quite* extraordinary! But I've never seen a Throne
like this in my life! And what on earth is a valuable
Hooligan Throne doing miles out here, abandoned
on a beach in the Uglithug Territories? It's ini... ini...
what do I mean to say, Hiccup?'

'Inexplicable,' said Hiccup, peering rather
cautiously at the Throne.

There was something about this Throne that gave
him the spooks.

Maybe it was the faint impression of a
blood-stain on the back of it. A very old

blood-stain, washed in the waters of the ocean for some time, but still there, a faint brown flower, the memory of some ancient betrayal.

'I think it must have been washed up by the storm, like all these other things,' said Hiccup, gesturing to a whole load of driftwood and bits of old bottles and jugs and crabshells and axe-handles and half of a fish-box that lay drowning in pools of water in the sand on the beach.

'But what a Treasure!' breathed Stoick the Vast, cheering up tremendously. 'And it belongs to US! It must have been some Hooligan Chieftain's Throne back in the old days!'

Well, well, well! It was worth holing *The Fat Penguin* for this. Stoick rubbed his hands together excitedly.

Stoick's present Throne back on Berk hadn't really been the same since Toothless accidentally set fire to it a couple of months ago.*

It was hard to impress with a Throne that had only three legs.

'OK, Warriors!' Stoick yelled. 'Haul the thing above the high-tide mark and then let's get the supper on and have an early night!

'Now, Hiccup,' Stoick continued, 'you will learn

---

* Please read *A Hero's Guide to Deadly Dragons*.

the importance of Making the Best of Things, another
very important Hooligan characteristic. This may
not be such a bad camping spot after all. Look! No
jellyfish! Perfectly sheltered! Plenty of lookout areas!
LET'S SET UP CAMP OVER BY THAT FAT
ROCK WITH THE RUNES ON IT, GUYS!'

Stoick stomped off up the beach towards a large
rock covered in UG runes.

'What do the runes say, Hiccup?' asked Fishlegs
nervously.

Hiccup knelt down beside the rock.
'They say, "Trespassers will be Killed
Horribly but Mercifully Quickly if they
are Lucky." That's the gist of it
anyway. UG runes are very
difficult to read.'

'PSHAW!'
shouted Stoick

the Vast, throwing down a whole heap of driftwood for the campfire. 'The Uglithugs very rarely come to this beach because of the whole, you know, *haunting* thing.

Hiccup had this horrible feeling that the Throne was like an evil Creature, and it was trying to suck him in.

So if you think about it, this *could* be the Perfect Camping Spot. They'll never find us here!'

The Hairy Hooligans moved the Throne and built the fire on a heap of stones and driftwood on the beach, and roasted and ate some mackerel for supper. Then they rolled themselves up in their bearskins around the fire, their hunting-dragons lying beside them, and tried to get to sleep.

Which wasn't easy.

For, as the Hooligans found out, there may have been ANOTHER reason why the Uglithugs didn't visit the Beach of the

Broken Heart much.

For the mild humming and drumming that had been coming from the black silhouette of the Island of Berserk to the south earlier in the evening got louder and louder as the stars came out. The drums beat out a war-like tribal beat that seemed to dance a tattoo in time to Hiccup's racing heart.

And as the moon rose, a truly terrible, unearthly sound rose from out of that island.

A ghostly ghastly HOWLING is the only way to describe it, like the howling of hungry wolves. But only a human throat could make that noise, or *half* a human anyway.

The dreadful sound slipped down Hiccup's spine like an icy trickle of water.

'Berserks…' came the deep voice of Stoick the Vast from out of the darkness on the other side of the fire. He tutted disapprovingly. 'They're still very keen on their Human Sacrifices I'm afraid. So old-fashioned. That reminds me. My father always used to say: "Never invade a major land-mass at the beginning of the winter and NEVER go to Berserk." Remember that, Hiccup,' he said importantly. 'That's a fine piece of fatherly advice.'

'Oh don't worry, I'll remember that,' Hiccup whispered back.

'I know I shouldn't be criticising your father, but this really is NOT the perfect camping spot,' moaned Fishlegs, shivering in his bearskin beside Hiccup. 'We're sleeping on a haunted beach, trespassing on the territory of the most brutal and suspicious Chief in the Barbaric World, and a whole load of weirdos are having a Ceremony of Human Sacrifice on the island next door. I'm not generally in favour of sleeping out anyway, but this really is the worst-case scenario…'

Eventually, one by one, the Hooligans dropped off to sleep. Hiccup was the last, staring at the stars, and at the flickering dying of the firelight. He was wondering where Camicazi was. He was feeling fairly frightened himself, but at least he wasn't alone.

Four hours later, he sat bolt upright as an electrifying scream ripped across the beach.

'Berserks...' grumbled Stoick, groaning as he rolled in the sand, pulling his bearskin over his head. 'Unpleasant, but no threat at that distance...'

The Hooligans and their dragons, who had all sat upright as one at the sound of that scream, settled themselves back down again.

But Hiccup didn't lie down immediately. He was looking at something.

Beyond the firelight, where the Throne sat quiet in the darkness.

Oh stark mad Berserks and lunatic ghost-ladies! *There was* somebody SITTING *in the Throne!*

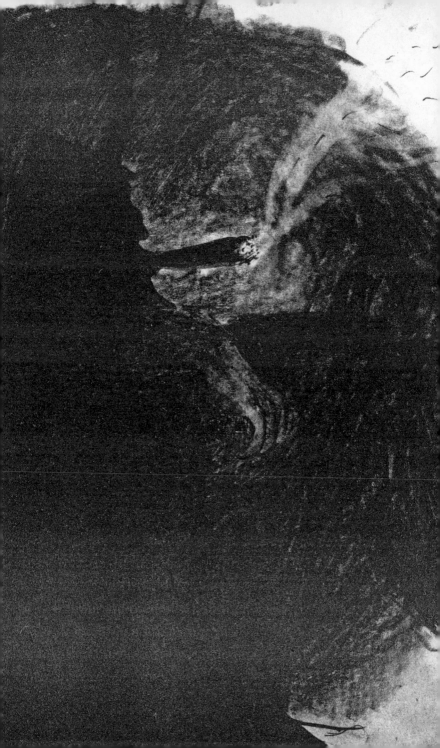

3. DEFINITELY NOT THE PERFECT CAMPING SPOT

It could only be one of three things really.

It could be the Ghost-Lady of the Beach come for their hearts.

It could be a Berserk looking for another human to sacrifice.

Or it could be an Uglithug wanting to kill them Horribly but Mercifully Quickly if they were Lucky.

All *three* of those things were worth a pretty good scream, a real belter in fact, and Hiccup opened up his mouth.

But a great hairy hand closed over it.

Hiccup could only watch with terrified, popping eyes as quiet dark shadowy figures poured over the brow of the beach and positioned themselves silently behind every Hooligan's head.

The figure in the Throne was shrouded in darkness. Hiccup could see the magnificent stag-horned outline of his helmet against the night sky. He was slowly smoking a

cigar* that glowed bright in the moonlight. He made a motion with his hand, and every Hooligan around that campfire was awoken with a knife to his throat.

Every Hooligan except for Stoick.

Stoick snored on, regardless.

The figure seated in the Throne got up and strolled towards the sleeping Stoick. He gave him a gentle kick.

Stoick the Vast snatched the bearskin blanket from his head and sat up indignantly. 'Wossat? Who's there?'

He made a sleepy grab for his axe.

The horned figure made another slight gesture with his hand, and quiet shadowy figures drew the Throne closer to the Fire.

'UG *the Uglithug! What are* YOU *doing here?*' gulped Stoick the Vast, his axe already drooping in his hand in dismay that all of his Warriors had knives held at their throats.

Stoick the Vast was a little slow on the uptake, but even *he* could see it didn't look good.

They were on Uglithug land, and the chewed bones of Uglithug mackerel were littered all around their campfire.

'Well you know, Stoick,' purred UG the Uglithug.

---

* Smoking was a common practice in the Americas at this time, but highly unusual for a Viking. UG bought his cigars from 'a little man up north'. See *How to Ride a Dragon's Storm* for Viking relations with America.

His smile was the smile of a tiger being friendly. 'It *is* MY beach...'

Most of the Chieftains Hiccup had come across were tough but a little dim.

UG was scary because he was not only the most powerful and brutal King in the Barbaric World, whose territories stretched so far that a dragon could fly east for a week and never reach the end of them, he was also highly intelligent.

'I can explain, UG!' gasped Stoick the Vast.

'Live and let live is my philosophy, Stoick,' smiled UG the Uglithug. 'All you Chieftains out there in the wild west are burglars. If *you* want to burgle each other, and raid each other, and murder each other, do I interfere? I do not. As long as you don't try and burgle ME,' said UG, who had stopped laughing with terrible abruptness and now spoke with pure menace, 'because then that *is* my business. If anyone tries to burgle ME, then...' UG let the sentence trail off suggestively.

'... Then you kill them Horribly,' said Stoick eagerly, pleased he now knew what UG was talking about, 'but Mercifully Quickly if they're Lucky. Yes, I know that, UG...'

'Well done, Stoick, well done,' said UG. 'I'm glad to hear it. But you see, Stoick, my Spy-dragons tell me that you have come here, uninvited, in the middle of the night, with all your army…' He gestured at Stoick's ships with his cigar. 'A *suspicious* man might say that by planting your Throne on my beaches you are laying claim to my lands. *Some* people might say that wasn't very friendly…'

'No, no, UG, it isn't like that!' blustered Stoick the Vast. 'That isn't my Throne! We just found it lying here on the beach!'

UG the Uglithug smiled, and it wasn't a pretty sight. 'You are an old friend, Stoick,' said UG, and now his voice had hardened to ice, 'but even your friends would say that you have never been the brightest barbarian in the business. If it *isn't* your Throne, why is the Hooligan coat of arms plastered all over the back of it?'

UG leant back in the Throne and jammed his cigar back between his teeth. He lifted his arm. Hiccup could see that all the Uglithugs, their knives poised over the Hooligans' throats, had their eyes on that arm, and he knew that if UG's arm came down, they would all be executed on the spot.

Hiccup bit the finger of the brute who was covering his mouth, and shouted: 'BIG-BOOBIED BERTHA KNOWS WE ARE HERE!'

UG the Uglithug's cigar hovered thoughtfully in the air. 'Let the boy speak,' said UG the Uglithug at last.

The Uglithug holding Hiccup let him go, and he sprawled on the sand.

'And who,' said UG softly, 'is this?'

'This is my son and Heir, Hiccup Horrendous Haddock the Third,' said Stoick the Vast hurriedly.

'That's a very long name for a very small Heir,' said UG. 'And what do you have to say for yourself, Hiccup Horrendous Haddock the Third?'

'This is not a raid. We are out looking for Bertha's child who went missing in the Storm,' said Hiccup. 'That Throne, if you look at it closely, has been underwater for at least a hundred years. It must have belonged to one of our ancestors and been washed up by the storm. And Big-Boobied Bertha will ask some awkward questions if the entire Hooligan Tribe disappears while on a perfectly peaceful mission in Uglithug territory.'

UG the Uglithug looked carefully at Hiccup.

'I could tell her it was all a tragic mistake,' said UG the Uglithug, stroking his beard.

'Questions would be asked,' repeated Hiccup firmly. 'Suspicions would be raised. Bodies would be difficult to hide.'

'A *clever* little Hooligan,' said UG thoughtfully. 'A politician, in fact. In the Hooligan Tribe! Well, *there's* an interesting development.'

He smoked his cigar in the darkness of the evening for a moment or two.

UG the Uglithug spread wide his arms. 'I believe you, Stoick!' he shouted.

He shook Stoick heartily by the hand.

The entire Uglithug Tribe removed their knives from the Hooligans' throats and took a step back.

'*Do* you?' said Stoick, letting out a huge breath of relief, but slightly amazed.

'I DO!' bellowed UG. 'I WAS NEVER GOING TO KILL YOU! IT WAS JUST A JOKE!'

'A joke?' said Stoick.

'HA HA HA!' roared UG the Uglithug.

'Ha ha ha,' replied Stoick.

'HA HA HA HA HA,' roared the Uglithugs and the Hooligans, some of them more heartily than others.

'I HAD A COMPLETELY DIFFERENT REASON FOR COMING DOWN HERE TO SPEAK TO YOU! ISN'T THAT FUNNY?' laughed UG the Uglithug.

'Very funny,' said Stoick awkwardly. 'Erm…
what reason is that then, UG?'

'Well, it's very serious actually, Stoick,' said UG,
sobering up. 'I hope we're going to be able to sort it
out without blood being spilt. But I doubt it.'

Stoick swallowed. 'Oh dear. That *does* sound
serious.'

'It concerns the honour of my daughter,' said UG
the Uglithug, very seriously indeed. 'Someone from
the Hooligan Tribe has been sending her love letters.'

Stoick's heart would have plummeted down to
his boots if he had been wearing any.

Back in those dark old ages, sending people love
letters was a:

Very.

Serious.

And.

Deadly.

Matter.

INDEED.

'Shall we
discuss the problem
over tea?' smiled UG
the Uglithug.

UH-
OH.

4. TEA WITH UG THE UGLITHUG

'*Tea?*' said Stoick in a slightly dazed way. 'But it's the middle of the night!'

'From the sound of the Berserks I should say it was about three o'clock in the morning,' said UG the Uglithug. 'They don't really get going with their Dead-of-Night Ceremony until two. Interesting choice of camping spot, by the way, Stoick…'

'It isn't *perfect*,' Stoick admitted gloomily.

The horrible howling from the Isle of Berserk intensified, at a pitch that made goosebumps creep up on the arms as if you were being stroked by nettles and the individual hairs on the back of your neck go shooting upwards like the tentacles on a spiny sea urchin.

'Let's say… *ten* to three,' amended UG the Uglithug, cocking his head as he listened to the noise.

'Whatever,' said Stoick. 'It's quite late for tea. And I've already eaten.'

'Oh but I *insist*,' smiled UG the Uglithug. 'Just a picnic, you know, Stoick. A little ten-to-three snack, to welcome you to the Uglithug lands. It's always better to have a difficult conversation over a spot of food.'

He clapped his hands.

UG's boat was moored beside the broken down *The Fat Penguin*, and from it the grinning Uglithugs brought out plates and spoons and glasses of mead and hunks of deer and milk and bread and everything you might need for a little snack at ten to three in the morning.

Toothless had not had supper with everybody else earlier, because he had been so tired on account of missing his two naps. He had fallen asleep *while eating*, poor Toothless, just nodded off with his head in the soup, and Hiccup had washed his face and snuggled him up in his waistcoat rather than disturb him. He had slept right through the howling horrifying sound of the Berserk Dead-of-Night Ceremony, and the subsequent Uglithug attack.

It was only now that he smelt food that he put his little snuffling nose outside Hiccup's waistcoat and opened bleary eyes.

'F-f-foooò!' said Toothless with little whimpers of excitement, instantly drooling, he was so hungry. 'Toothless s-s-s-starving!'

'Now, Toothless, *calmly*,' warned Hiccup, holding the haddock up to him on a spoon, 'I know you're hungry but don't eat it all at once... it always gives

55

you a tummy-ache… slowly, Toothless…
little bites… slowly… TOOTHLESS!'

Too late.

So keen was greedy little Toothless,
so hungry was he from flying all over the
coves looking for Camicazi, that he not
only gobbled up the haddock in one, eager
gulp…

… he also ate the spoon.

'Oh, *Toothless*,' sighed Hiccup, breaking off as he
saw that UG the Uglithug's daughter was joining them
for the meal.

Hiccup had caught a glimpse of her before, at
the Annual Games, surrounded by bodyguards.

'This is my dear little daughter, Tantrum
O'UGerly,' said UG the Uglithug.

UG's dear little daughter Tantrum was about six
foot two with a lot of flame-red hair and green eyes.
A beautiful red Snaredragon had made a nest on her
head and she was feeding it acorns.

She looked spectacularly beautiful and
spectacularly cross.

'Oh for Thor's sake…' squeaked Fishlegs,
blushing absolutely scarlet, 'she's looking at us…
she's smiling at us… she's *waving* at us! Act

56

natural… act cool… nobody panic…'

Fishlegs turned first red, then white,
and was so overcome with the emotion
of the moment that he fainted dead
away, and fell off his chair.

'Oh, very cool, Fishlegs,' said
Hiccup, bringing him round and
helping him up to the table again,
'very suave. FAINTING always
impresses these Amazon Viking hell-
kittens. I have to hand it to you, you really know how
to wow the ladies. You'll be a real heart-breaker when
you get older.'

'Has she stopped looking at us?' asked Fishlegs,
with his eyes closed.

'Hang on a second… keep your eyes closed…
she's still laughing… *and* pointing…' said Hiccup.
'No… she's stopped now. She's picking her nose and
talking to her neighbour again. You're quite safe, you
can open your eyes.'

'She looked at me…' sighed Fishlegs, his hand
on his heart. 'Tantrum O'UGerly looked at me… and
smiled at me… and waved at me… She's an angel!
She's a goddess!'

Hiccup stared at Fishlegs as if he was crazy.
'What's the matter with you, Fishlegs, have you gone

bananas?' Hiccup checked Fishlegs's eyes for any Berserk tendencies. They tended to go a bit pink when he was in a Berserk kind of mood.

'My daughter means a lot to me, Stoick,' said UG, with a hint of menace in his tone. 'This is a question of honour and the Barbaric Code. You know the rules. Whoever writes love letters to a daughter *without* asking permission from the father, must instantly ask for her hand-in-marriage or it is an intolerable insult to *her* and to her *entire* Tribe.'

Now, in the Barbaric Archipelago, weirdly, one of the most dangerous things you could possibly do was to fall in LOVE. Strangely, it was far more risky than Dragon-riding, or swordfighting, or any of the other perilous pursuits that a young Viking undertook.

'However, as the rules clearly state,' said UG briskly, 'IF the person who wrote these letters is of Royal Blood, they can try and win my daughter's hand by completing a single Impossible Task of MY choosing.'

Ug's dear little daughter
Tantrum →

'And what if the letter-writer is NOT of Royal Blood?' asked Hiccup.

'Then they have insulted the Honour of the Uglithug Tribe and I get to kill them on the spot,' smiled UG the Uglithug. 'And if *nobody* owns up, I get to kill every unmarried young man in your Hooligan Tribe. All above board and within the Barbaric Code. No questions asked. No suspicious fingers pointed. All quite within my rights.'

'It's a bad business, this LOVE business,' said Stoick, gloomily shaking his head. 'A very bad business.'

'But you've forgotten one small important point, UG,' said Hiccup. 'You can't *prove* that any of us wrote those letters.'

'It's very unlikely,' said Stoick proudly. 'Most of us Hooligans can't actually write.'

UG smiled. He shoved his cigar into his mouth and stood up. 'I shall read one of the letters, just in case it jogs the memory of anybody here today.'

The mighty barbaric Chieftain got to his feet.

The poetry of the moment was slightly lost by the fact that it was being read by the most brutal Chieftain in the Barbaric World smoking a large cigar, his eyes twinkling with wickedness.

the Berk Bog-Rose
(stings like a stinging
nettle scent of a
cow pat)

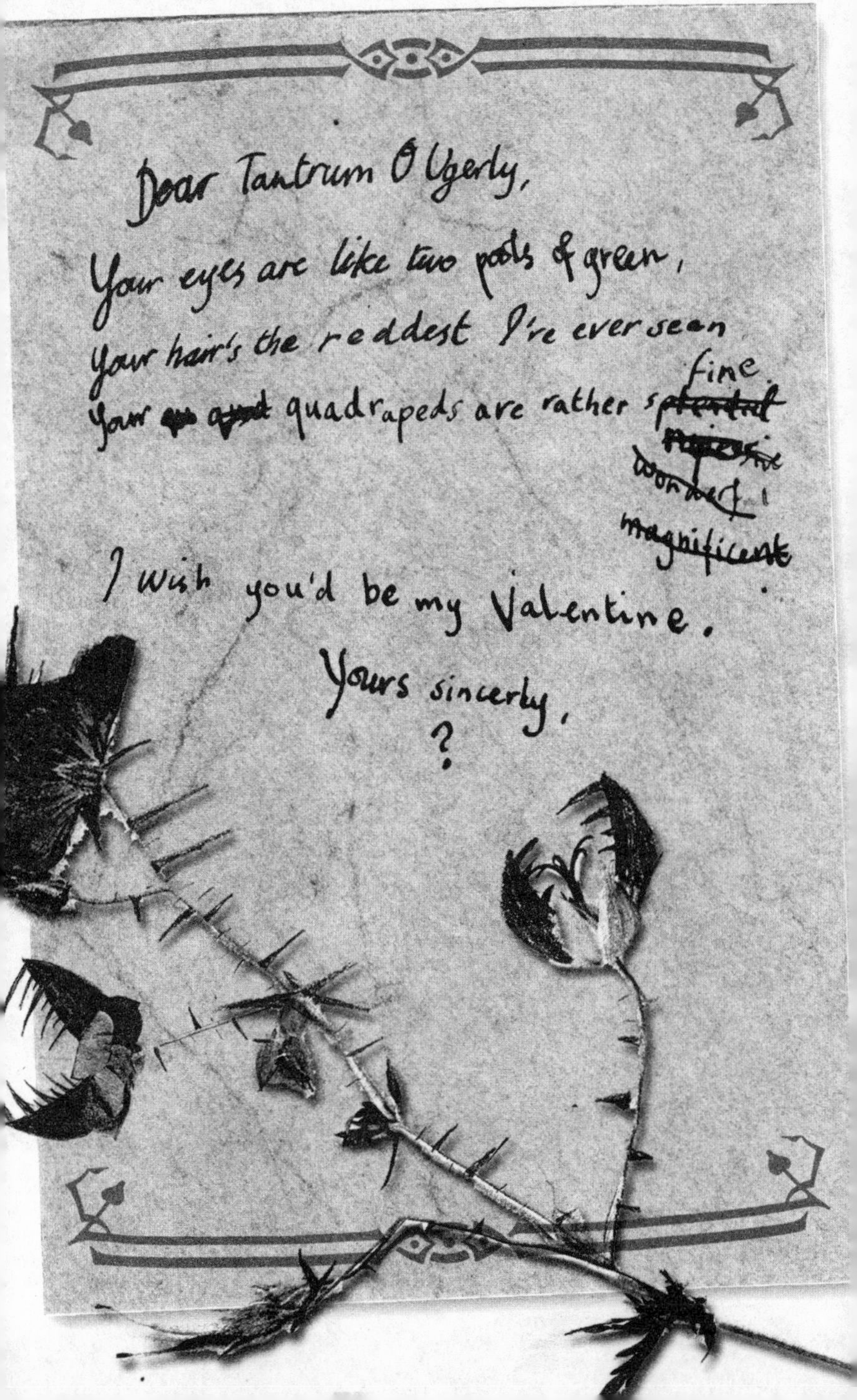

Dear Tantrum O'Ugerly,

Your eyes are like two pools of green,
Your hair's the reddest I've ever seen
Your ~~and~~ quadrapeds are rather ~~splendid~~ fine
~~rather nice~~
~~wonderful~~
magnificent

I wish you'd be my Valentine.

Yours sincerly,

?

The Hooligans roared with laughter.

'Are they laughing at my daughter?' asked UG mildly.

'SILENCE!' roared Stoick. There was silence on the beach, apart from the odd snigger, hastily stifled. Tantrum O'UGerly admired her reflection in a golden cup in a furious sort of way.

'I'm waiting for someone to own up...' said UG the Uglithug... and then Hiccup turned to whisper something to Fishlegs and he caught sight of Fishlegs's face. Fishlegs was bright red. He was shifting nervously in his chair, and he wouldn't meet Hiccup's eye.

A horrible thought struck Hiccup. UG smiled an incredibly nasty smile. 'There's a pressed flower sent with it... a romantic touch, don't you think? Very sweet...' UG said softly, shaking the letter so that the flower fell into his hand. 'And here it is... the Berk Bog-Rose.'

The Berk Bog-Rose was brown, and prickly, and it ponged a bit (alas, not in a good way). But it was very rare... so rare, in fact, that the only place it grew was in the boggiest bits of the bogs of Berk, and it had thus become the tribal flower of the Hooligans.

UG sat down again. 'I'll leave you to talk among yourselves.'

5. THE TWELFTH FIANCÉ OF TANTRUM O'UGERLY

Hiccup turned to Fishlegs in horror.

'It wasn't *you*, was it Fishlegs?' he hissed desperately at his friend.

Of course it couldn't have been... Fishlegs was only thirteen and a quarter. He was *far* too young to be sending love poetry to beautiful sulky princesses with homicidal maniacs for fathers...

But Fishlegs was redder than a sunset. He pushed his glasses further on to his nose, and mumbled so low that Hiccup could barely hear him.

'Um...' he coughed. 'I've been practising my poetry, you see. It's quite a good poem, don't you think?' said Fishlegs, proud of his artistic effort, despite the peril of the moment. 'Although the word "quadraped" is not very poetic... I had some trouble with it... poetry isn't as easy as it looks...'

'What are you talking about, you loon?' hissed Hiccup. 'Who cares if it's a good poem or not? Uglithugs are not exactly particular about their poetry. They're much better at removing people's heads and tying their arms in complicated reef knots. The thing is, why in Woden's name did you send her the beastly poem in the first place?'

Fishlegs was now whiter than a piece of paper. 'I just thought she was quite pretty, and so she was inspiring my poetry. The thing is,' explained Fishlegs, 'I'm not sure whether the whole Hooligan Warrior, swords-and-axes, grunting-and-thumping thing is really working out for me. So I was just thinking that if I *failed* the Training Programme which let's face it is quite likely, I could always start out as a poet, make my way up to being a wandering minstrel, maybe end up as a BARD, even...'

'It's a good idea, Fishlegs, I'm not knocking it,' said Hiccup, 'but let's talk about your career options later. *Now* we have a problem.'

'I'm sorry, Hiccup,' said Fishlegs.

Fishlegs took his glasses off and put them on again in a harassed sort of way.

He swallowed hard.

'What do you think he's going to do to me?' he whispered back to Hiccup.

'He's going to kill you,' Hiccup explained patiently. 'Horribly but Mercifully Quickly if you're Lucky.'

'You think so?' said Fishlegs quaveringly.

'I not only think so, I know so,' said Hiccup. 'To even GET to be one of her fiancés in the first place

you have to be of ROYAL BLOOD.
I'm afraid we are living in prejudiced
times, and by my reckoning that
means death-on-the-spot for you.'

'OK,' smiled UG, 'I'm afraid
I'm going to have to ask the culprit
to own up. I'll count to five. One...
two... three...'

'I have to own up,' Fishlegs
whispered. 'Or else we'll ALL get
killed. It's been nice knowing you,
Hiccup.'

'... *four*...' said UG warningly.

Fishlegs got unsteadily to his
feet, and shakily wiped his steamed-
up glasses on his shirtfront, before
jamming them back on his nose with
determination.

'Wait!' Hiccup whispered. 'I
think I may have a plan!'

'A clever one?' replied Fishlegs
hopefully.

'Oh for Thor's sake,' said
Hiccup. 'Clever-*ish*. There's no
time to be fussy...'

'STOP!' yelled Hiccup.

Oh, for Thor's sake... You really owe me for this one, Fishlegs...

65

Everyone turned round and looked at him.

Oh brother.

This was going to be hard.

'*I* wrote the poem,' said Hiccup.

There was a short, astonished silence.

Hiccup couldn't look at Snotlout or Dogsbreath the Duhbrain, who were beside themselves with glee.

'YOUR HEIR wrote the poem, Stoick,' chuckled UG the Uglithug, leaning back in the Throne and taking a good long puff on his cigar. 'I KNEW there'd be a happy ending.'

'Hiccup!' cried Stoick the Vast. 'YOU didn't write this letter, did you?'

'I'm afraid so, Father,' lied Hiccup.

SNORT SNORT SNORT went Snotlout and Dogsbreath the Duhbrain.

'What does this mean?' said Stoick the Vast, trying to take it in.

'It means,' drawled UG the Uglithug, very, very pleased with himself, 'that according to our Barbaric Code, your son Hiccup Horrendous Haddock the Third, being of Royal Blood, has had the excellent good luck to become the latest Fiancé of my dearly beloved daughter, Princess Tantrum O'UGerly.'

'But... but... but...' blustered Stoick the Vast,

trying to focus on just one of the reasons that he felt that this was a gob-smackingly bad idea. 'What about the age gap?'

'I don't think you'll find the age gap is a problem,' grinned UG the Uglithug. 'To actually MARRY my daughter, he would have to pass the Impossible Task that I set.'

'You said the "latest" Fiancé,' said Hiccup. 'How many Fiancés have you actually HAD, Princess Tantrum?'

'Eleven,' said Tantrum, tossing her hair and throwing her father a look so furious that his beard should have gone up in flames on the spot. 'That's counting the Fiancé-Before-the-Fiancé-Before-Last, who is the one I love and am actually going to marry...'

'*Love!*' sneered UG the Uglithug. 'A princess can't marry for LOVE! Besides, I am not sure that the Fiancé-Before-the-Fiancé-Before-Last really *counts* because I think he was lying about his Royal Blood.'

'I am not going to marry somebody just because they have stay-at-home *Royal Blood*, Father!' stormed Tantrum. 'I am sick of castles and roofs and bodyguards and jewels. *I* am going to marry a HERO. I am going to marry *my* Hero, and sail into the sunset, and sleep under the stars, and live by the sword, and let our boat take us wherever the wind blows us. *I* am going to marry *my* Hero, the Fiancé-Before-the-Fiancé-Before-Last, who is the one I love!'

'Yes, well there's a tiny problem about that, isn't there, Tantrum?' smiled UG the Uglithug. 'Your Hero never returned from the Impossible Task… If he was a *true* Hero, he would have returned.'

'He *will* return…' said Tantrum stubbornly, tossing her beautiful hair and crossing her arms. 'He *will* return. I'm waiting for him.'

'Of course you can wait, Tantrum my dear,' said UG the Uglithug. 'But you may be waiting a long time. You may be waiting for ever.'

'I can wait a long time,' said Tantrum. 'I can wait for ever.'

'Well, you just keep on waiting,' cooed UG the Uglithug. 'Don't let me stop you. In the meantime,' he turned to Stoick the Vast, '*my* only criteria for my daughter Tantrum's hand-in-marriage is Royal Blood…' ('HA!' snorted Tantrum and tossed her hair.) '… and for the Fiancé to provide one barrel of mead for the honeymoon.'*

Stoick the Vast cheered up like anything. 'Is THAT the Impossible Task?' he said eagerly. 'That

---

* 'Honeymoon' is a Viking expression. The term comes from the month of partying with mead, a drink made from honey, to celebrate a marriage.

doesn't sound Impossible at all! The
Impossible Task *I* had to complete when *I*
got married was far harder than that. I had to
fetch the Fire-Stone from Lava-Lout Mountain,
and that was quite tricky, I can tell you. It required
strength, agility, huge muscles, real Hero qualities!
This sounds easy-peasy in comparison! ONE barrel of
mead is nothing!'

'I'm sure there's a catch,' said Hiccup.
'Otherwise eleven previous Fiancés wouldn't have
failed the task.'

'No catch,' shrugged UG. 'But only the best is
good enough for us Uglithugs. The mead has to be
made from the best honey in the world. And the bees
that make the best honey in the world...'

UG paused for effect.

'... are the bees of BERSERK.'

There was silence around the campfire on the
Beach of the Broken Heart.

The moon's path glittered down on the soft
lapping waves, and the mirrored silhouettes of the
boats moored in the Bay danced in the starlight.

In the marshes behind, the Neverbirds were
calling that haunting cry of theirs that sounded like:
'Where *are* yo-o-o-u? Where *are* yo-o-o-ou?'

And everybody around that campfire turned to the great hulking brutish silhouette of the island of Berserk, to the south. Like a bent-over beast it was, brooding with misery and longing on the skyline. And, as if on cue, the Dead-of-Night Ceremony came to an end, with a great crescendo of howling, like a thousand wailing Furies with a toothache, and the tops of the trees of Berserk swayed, although there was no wind to sway them.

What was HAPPENING out there?

Hiccup really, *really* didn't want to find out.

Stoick the Vast sat up to his full, proud height. He put a hand on Hiccup's shoulder. 'MY SON will collect this honey from the bees of Berserk, or DIE in the attempt! Isn't that right, Hiccup?'

'That's right,' said Hiccup, swallowing hard.

'That's just what I wanted to hear!' roared UG the Uglithug. 'How about Midsummer's Day for the wedding? That gives you plenty of time to di— er – collect lots of honey. So I'll expect you at Uglithug Castle, Midsummer morning, five o'clock sharp, with ooh... say... five pots of Beserk honey? RIGHT,' UG rubbed his hands together with satisfaction, 'I think that covers everything. You won't mind if I take this Throne with me, will you, Stoick? Anything that drifts on to this beach belongs to ME.'

Before the Uglithugs left, Hiccup had one more question for his future father-in-law.

'Camicazi,' he said, 'the Bog-Burglar we are looking for. Have you seen her, Your Ugliness?'

'Well,' said UG. 'Is Camicazi a small blonde child, so high, with hair that needs a brush and a terrible habit of trespassing on my land and stealing beautiful rare Mood-dragons that don't belong to her? Only UG the Uglithug can own a Mood-dragon, and anyone who steals from ME will be taught a terrible lesson.'

'That's her,' said Hiccup, getting that awful sinking feeling again.

'Then I've never seen her before in my life,' said UG with one of his particularly grim smiles. 'Goodbye, Hiccup Horrendous Haddock the Third.'

He also ate the spoon.

6. ALL ALONE

Meanwhile, somewhere not
so far away, Camicazi was
singing to herself in the dark.
She was singing to keep
her spirits up.

Camicazi was not the
kind of child who panicked in a
difficult situation.

This was lucky, because
she had been imprisoned in total
blackness for a week now, in the
suffocating claustrophobic confines
of a tree trunk so narrow that she
could reach out and touch the
walls of her cell on either side.

And the only lock could
not be picked, she knew
that now. And there was
nothing to dig with and
nowhere to dig to.

But *she* was not
afraid, she told herself.
She was scared for her
dragon, Stormfly, of course,
who had been taken away
by that horrid man and put
who knows where? Camicazi
hoped that Stormfly had not been
locked up too, for Stormfly could
not bear confinement.

But she herself, *she*,
Camicazi, was not afraid.

Even though nobody who
loved her knew where she was.
The tree in which she was
imprisoned was in the middle of
a forest. And from the *outside*,
there was nothing about the
tree that distinguished it
from the other 35,672
trees standing

immediately around it. And she could not be more utterly and comprehensively and mind-losingly lost, than if she had been steering *The Stormy Petrel* across a tempest-tossed night sky, and accidentally dropped down a black hole in space.

But I am not *really* lost, she said to herself, because it does not matter so much WHERE you are as long as you know WHO you are. And *she* was a Bog-Burglar, and Bog-Burglars do not scare easy.

That was why Camicazi started to sing the

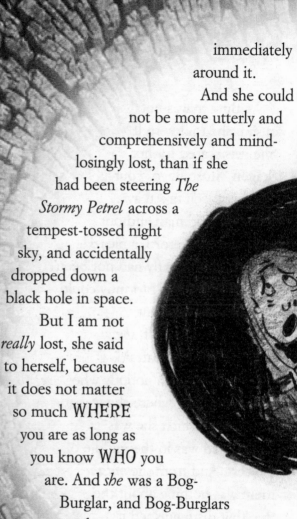

Bog-
Burglar
Tribal Anthem,
shouting it out as loudly
as she could in the echoing
blackness of the tree:

'BOG-BURGLARS KNOW
NOT THE MEANING
OF FEAR! FOR BOG-
BURGLAR HEARTS
ARE STRONGER THAN
OAK! YOUR SHIP IS
NOT LOST WHEN THE
SEA IS YOUR
HOME! AND BOG-
BURGLARS... FIGHT...
FOREVER!'

Loud and defiant were
the words, ringing out boldly
within the hollowness of the tree,
comforting Camicazi with every
heartening echo.

But *outside* the tree...
Why, *outside* the tree
they could not be
heard at all.

7. I'M GETTING MARRIED IN THE MORNING

The Hooligans mended *The Fat Penguin*, and carried on with the fruitless search for Camicazi for a day or so more (this time being very careful to camp on the Island of the Quiet Life, in a camping-spot with loads of jellyfish but no ghosts, Berserks or Uglithugs).

Stoick the Vast then sent a Carrier-dragon to Big-Boobied Bertha with the sad news that they couldn't find Camicazi anywhere, and they returned home to Berk.

UG the Uglithug hadn't said that Hiccup had to collect the honey *all on his own*, so Stoick the Vast decided that the chances of the Quest to Collect Honey from the Island of Berserk being successful would be greatly improved if all the Warriors in the Hooligan Tribe joined Hiccup in a midnight Dragon-riding raid on the island.

So this is why the next evening all twelve Vikings

on the Warrior Training Programme were standing
to attention in a raggedy line in front of Gobber the
Belch, the teacher in charge of the Pirate Training
Programme on Berk, dressed in their black night-time
flying gear, in front of the Almost Wood around Huge
Hill, the highest point on Berk.

'LISTEN UP, GUYS!' roared Gobber the
Belch, 'on account of young Hiccup here being a
Fiancé...'

Jeers and smoochy noises from the line.

'Hiccup and Tantrum up a tree...
K-I-S-S-I-N-G...' taunted Clueless, an ignorant young
bruiser with ears that stuck out like a jug.

'Hey, Hiccup, what's it like to be in lu-u-urve...?'
sneered Tuffnut Junior.

'Your eyes are like two pools of
green... Your hair's the reddest
I've ever seen,' chanted
Speedifist.

'HA HA HA HA
HA!' Everybody roared
with laughter, as
Hiccup turned blood
scarlet.

'I don't see why

First comes LU-U-R-VE...
Then comes MA-RRIAGE...
Then comes the
baby in a
baby
Carriage!

we **ALL** have to risk our lives just because the Useless is weak enough to fall in lu-u-urve...' sneered Snotlout. 'He should be ashamed of himself, writing poetry that soppy... and his poetry is pants!'

'SILENCE!' yelled Gobber. 'This is a good chance to practise your Dragon-riding skills, Snotlout. Now, Berserk is one of the most dangerous places in the Archipelago, because Berserks are the most terrifying Warriors in the world. We must avoid capture at all costs. So you will be riding your dragon **AT SPEED** in the darkness while trying to avoid trees. Not as easy as it sounds.'

The young Warriors hadn't been Dragon-riding in the air for long.

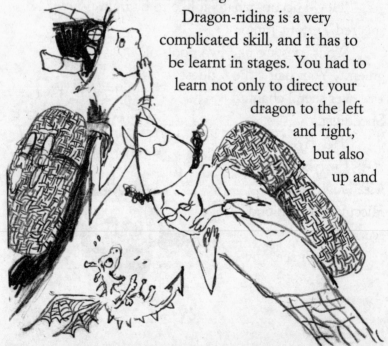

Dragon-riding is a very complicated skill, and it has to be learnt in stages. You had to learn not only to direct your dragon to the left and right, but also up and down vertically through the air, often at extraordinary speed. Dragons are such magnificent flyers that it takes years to master gliding, diving, flying backwards, flying in formation, looping the loop, and all the other aeronautic stunts that a dragon performs naturally in the wild.

'NOW!' roared Gobber. 'This is a training exercise! I have hung gourds from the trees to represent honey that you have to collect. You have to weave through the trees, collecting as much honey as you can, and then return here to the finishing line. Meanwhile *I* will be pretending to be a Poison-Darting-Scarer-cum-Berserk.'*

'Nice disguise, sir,' said Fishlegs.

'Thank you, Fishlegs,' said Gobber.

Gobber the Belch's Berserk disguise consisted of covering himself in war paint and putting a large pair of his own furry underpants on his head. He was

---

* Poison Darters and Scarers were dangerous dragons that were known to be living in the Berserk Forest.

carrying a bow loaded with arrows tipped with sticky blue woad.

'Now,' said Gobber, frowning pompously. 'If I catch you, or you get hit by one of these arrows, you can consider yourself deader than dodos if you were in a real-life Berserk Honey-Collecting Situation.' He cleared his throat. 'ON TO YOUR DRAGONS!' roared Gobber the Belch.

Hiccup's Riding-Dragon was an anxious, untidy Windwalker with raggedy ears and even more raggedy wings.

'Toothless got a tummy-ache,' whined Toothless. He WAS looking a little greener around the face than normal, but of course it was quite difficult to tell, because he was as green as the green green grass already, and he had just done five cartwheels in the air in a row, because he was feeling a little bored with all this TALKING going on.

'Well stop doing somersaults then,' Hiccup suggested.

'GO!!!!' roared Gobber, blasting on his horn.

Hiccup did all right in the exercise. The Windwalker was a little clumsy, but very fast at flying through the trees.

Poor old Fishlegs had some difficulties. His

Chickenpoxer was a cross little thing and reared around all the time, trying to buck Fishlegs off. Not to mention the fact that Fishlegs was allergic to it, so kept sneezing like a maniac.

And then Gobber, who was really enjoying himself, his red pork-pie face screaming like a banshee underneath those ridiculous furry underpants, sneaked up behind Fishlegs and let out an ear-splitting, rib-cracking, head-ringing HOWL that would have done credit to a REAL Poison Darter, Scarer or Berserk.

'*Aiiiiiiiiiiiieeeeeeeeeeee!*' screeched Fishlegs and with a cross little Shetland-pony snort the Chickenpoxer careered wildly out of control through the Almost Wood, ploughing through branches and narrowly avoiding bushes and completely flattening a tender young rowan tree that had survived the Great Storm by a whisker, and eventually charging head-first SPLAT into the trunk of a really-quite-sturdy

Arrow used by Vikings for training purposes. Note the wooden tip dipped in stinky woad.

81

oak like a small
apopleptic suicidal rhino.

Luckily Chickenpoxers
have heads built like crash-
helmets, so all that happened to
the Chickenpoxer was that he saw a
few stars.

Meanwhile, Fishlegs
s-a-a-a-a-a-a-ailed

over the top of the Chickenpoxer's
head, bonked his own head on the
tree, and then swung
 upside down from his
  safety-loop on the
   saddle of
    the dazed

Chickenpoxer, who went on flying distractedly through the air like a drunken moth.

Gobber the Belch caught up with them, yelling at the top of his bellow, and tactfully added insult to injury by shooting Fishlegs with arrows from his ankles to the tip of the lump on his head.

'That means I have hit you eighteen times over, Fishlegs!' yelled Gobber the Belch joyfully. 'You'll have to do better than THAT, boy,' he bellowed, before whirling around his dragon and shot after Tuffnut Junior, who swerved neatly through a copse of alders as if he were slaloming on skis.

'HA HA HA HA HA HA HA HA!' Several not

very sensitive young
Hooligans-in-Training pulled up
their dragons and stopped to laugh
at poor Fishlegs, swinging from the
Chickenpoxer's saddle.

It was of course *highly* amusing, but since Fishlegs
was dangling head down nearly thirty feet up in the air,
it was also a tad dangerous, so Hiccup gave the reins of
the Windwalker a shake and swooped down and caught
him just as his foot slipped out of the safety loop.

Hiccup flew Fishlegs down to the ground and
safety.

But Fishlegs had a recurring problem. His
Berserk tendencies often kicked in when he was
angry. When he was hit on the head, it
exaggerated the problem. And that was what
happened now.

So instead of *thanking* Hiccup, Fishlegs turned a
bright shade of puce and jumped up and down in a wild
shaking fury, screaming insults up at the laughing boys
on their dragons.

Which of course only made them laugh the
louder.

Worried, Hiccup dismounted the Windwalker and
tried to calm Fishlegs down by taking him by the arm.
'Hang on there, Fishlegs…'

Which was a mistake, because Fishlegs turned on him and shook off the arm in an extremity of rage, shouting, '*Will* you stop INTERFERING?'

'I only interfered,' said Hiccup soothingly, 'to stop you falling thirty feet on to your head...'

'You're ALWAYS interfering!' yelled Fishlegs. 'You INTERFERED when you said that you wrote those poems I spent ages writing!'

'I did that so that UG the Uglithug wouldn't murder you on the spot!' said Hiccup, really worried about Fishlegs now.

'HA! The real reason is that you think I'm not GOOD ENOUGH for a real princess, don't you?' howled Fishlegs.

Hiccup opened his mouth to say that wasn't the real reason at all but Fishlegs carried on. 'And you are, because you are of ROYAL BLOOD. And *I'm* just a Nobody, aren't I? I'm just a Nobody, from Nowhere, with no parents, who somebody found in the Harbour, and so the idea that I might end up with a beautiful princess like Tantrum is a *big joke*, isn't it?'

The boys on their dragons certainly thought it was a BIG JOKE. Snotlout laughed so hard he nearly fell off his dragon.

'Um,' said Gobber the Belch, 'I think perhaps

you ought to take Fishlegs home, Hiccup. He may
need a little lie-down. Take his dragon with you.'

And the others carried on practising, leaving
Hiccup with the Berserk Fishlegs.

'I do not need a little lie-down!' said Fishlegs,
punching the air in a barking-mad sort of way. 'I'M
PERFECTLY FINE!'

'That's right,' soothed Hiccup, 'but you got a
bonk on the head, and you've gone a little Berserk,
and you'll feel much better after a little lie-down…'

'But that's it!' said Fishlegs, stopping suddenly, his mouth falling open. 'Why didn't I think of this before? That's what I am! I'm a *Berserk*!'

That's 'it!
I'm a Berserk!

8. WHO ARE FISHLEGS'S PARENTS?

'Erm... what do you mean?' asked Hiccup.

'I *mean*,' Fishlegs said excitedly, 'that I was found as a baby inside this very lobster pot!' He removed the basket that he was carrying on his back and showed it to Hiccup.

'That's a rucksack,' said Hiccup.

'I made it into a rucksack,' explained Fishlegs, still bright red in the face and with that mad look in his eyes, 'because I didn't really need a lobster pot. I was found as a baby, inside *this actual lobster pot*. I drifted into the Harbour here, and somebody fished me out. And of course I must have sailed all the way from Berserk!'

'That's possible I suppose,' said Hiccup, considering it. 'But really it could have been ANYBODY who dropped you into the water. You have Berserk *tendencies*, that's not quite the same thing as being the full-blown, howling-at-the-moon, crazy-as-a-loon BERSERK...'

But Fishlegs wasn't listening, and he really DID look quite Berserk as he stood there yelling: 'I see now what I'm supposed to do! Fate is showing me the way here! This is a Quest in which I *finally* get to be the Hero... I'm going to go to Berserk RIGHT NOW, ALONE, and I'm going to fill this lobster pot with *five* pots of honey and then I'm going to come back here and nobody else will have to risk their lives, and won't that knock the smug smile off Snotlout's face. THEN everybody will stop laughing at me.'

Hiccup looked at Fishlegs, open-mouthed. 'But tonight it's a Full Moon! The Berserks will be right splat bang in the middle of a Dead-of-Night Ceremony!'

'Excellent!' said Fishlegs enthusiastically. 'I can join in!'

Hiccup said, soothingly, 'You know what, Fishlegs, I think Gobber was right. You need to

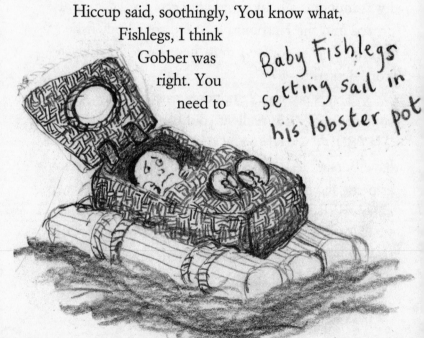

Baby Fishlegs setting sail in his lobster pot

The lobster claws found with Fishlegs as a baby. (He wears them as a necklace)

go home, and have a little lie-down.'

Fishlegs looked mutinous. 'You don't WANT me to go alone and be a Hero.'

'Of course I do...' said Hiccup, still in that soothing way, 'just not TONIGHT...'

So Hiccup took a cross, crazy Fishlegs home, and that appeared to be the end of the matter.

But much later, when Hiccup went to check if Fishlegs was feeling better, there was no sign of him. NO FISHLEGS. NO LOBSTER POT. NO CHICKENPOXER.

But there *was* a note addressed to Hiccup, put underneath a stone outside Fishlegs's front door.

Written in loopy, crazy, wild handwriting that indicated that the Berserk mood had not yet left Fishlegs.

Dear Hiccup,

I have gone to Berserk ~~&~~ alone
after all because this was **ALL my fault**
in the first place, and this is my chance to be
a Hero for once, and not a **BIG JoKe**

If I get caught by Berserks I think
they will not hurt me when I tell them
I am: family.

   Do NOT follow me.
   I can do this on my own.

        Best wishes,
         Fishlegs.

P.S. Give Dogsbreath and Dumbrain a big kiss
from me. I think my mother was
P.P.S.   a teapot.

'O Thor's Thumbnails.' Hiccup shifted anxiously from foot to foot. 'How can I not follow him? I should never have left him on his own! What am I going to DO?'

What *should* Hiccup have done?

Hiccup knew from bitter experience that if he went to his father, Stoick the Vast wouldn't think Fishlegs was important enough to risk the safety of the whole Tribe by going to Berserk on a Full Moon.

'I'll have to follow him to Berserk myself,' said Hiccup.

'NO, no no no no!' said Toothless, landing on Hiccup's head. 'N-n-not a good idea. You k-k-keep on not listening to me... Can we go home now, Toothless really got a tummy-ache...'

'Oh, I'm sorry, Toothless,' said Hiccup, 'I'm a little distracted because of Fishlegs...'

The reason for Toothless's tummy-ache became apparent when he attempted to flap off Hiccup's head, and couldn't do it. His tummy remained jammed to the helmet, and he just stuck there, flapping his wings wildly and squealing.

'What *are* you doing, Toothless?' asked Hiccup.

'Toothless s-s-stuck,' wailed Toothless.

Another clue that Fishlegs was still feeling a bit mad?

STOICK'S
VERY
IMPORTANT
AND
SPECIAL
MAGIC
STONE
WHICH
YOU
MUST
ON
NO
ACCOUNT
EVER
TOUCH
OR
PLAY
WITH ↓
DO
NOT
TOUCH ↑

Hiccup took off his helmet.
How extraordinary. Toothless's
tummy was, indeed, stuck to the
helmet.

'Toothless!' said Hiccup.
'You were playing in my father's
room this morning. You didn't
SWALLOW my father's magic
stone did you???!'*

Carefully, Hiccup pulled the
little dragon OFF his helmet and
cradled him in his arms.

'Wanted to see if it would
make Toothless m-m-magic...'
bleated Toothless in a small voice
pathetically. His big eyes filled with
tears. 'And now Toothless doesn't
f-f-feel very well!'

'Oh Toothless...' sighed
Hiccup. 'Spoons... magic stones...

Sniff sniff   Hmm... I wonder what THIS tastes like...

if people tell you not to do things, why do you always automatically go off and *do* them?'

Hiccup couldn't take Toothless back home because he didn't dare wait any longer to follow Fishlegs, so he took the honey-collecting jars out of the basket on his back, leaving them in a row outside Fishlegs's door. And then he tore out some heather from the ground, and put it in the bottom of the basket to make a nice springy bed for Toothless. The little dragon climbed in, groaning, and instantly fell asleep, curled up in a dragon sleeping-knot.

Toothless just stuck there, flapping his wings wildly

Hiccup put the basket back on his shoulders and got on to the Windwalker's back and took off into the sky, off to the island of Berserk.

---

* Stoick had brought a funny black stone back from an expedition to the north, which attracted metal things to it as if it were magic. They were absolutely forbidden to touch it, as the Hooligans did not know if it was harmful. The stone, of course, must have been a magnet.

"T-T-Toothless NOT
go in your father's study...
Toothless N-N-NOT play
with that funny magic
stone... Toothless N-N-NOT
wonder what it
taste like....Toothless
somewhere else at
the time..."

Poison Darters

~STATISTICS~

COLOURS: The dark green of the forest
ARMED WITH: Poison darts that knock the victim momentarily unconscious.
FEAR FACTOR:...........................7
ATTACK:.............................9
SPEED:...............................8
SIZE:.................................7
DISOBEDIENCE:......................9

Poison Darters shoot little arrows out of their mouths which carry venom that kills smaller animals and sends larger victims temporarily to sleep. They live in hollow tree trunks of the wilder forests of the Archipelago.

So this was how Hiccup found himself approaching the Woods That Howled on the back of the Windwalker at eleven o'clock in the evening on the night of a Full Moon.

The forests of the Dark Ages were a fearsome thing.

They were not pleasant airy little woods but great and terrible jungles, impenetrable in some parts, that spread over vast areas of the mainland to the east and were stalked by wolves, and bears, and wild men who fed on human flesh, and dragons so unspeakable that no one dared enter.

This was such a forest.

It was incredibly dark as they soared through the treetops, but the eye-beams of the Windwalker lit the way before them like searchlights. Great swarms of buzzing bees formed and re-formed in the eye-lights. Every now and then, they came across the startled black-and-white face of a Stink-dragon, or a Squirrelserpent, surrounded by a buzz of furious insects, its muzzle covered with honey.

At one point, the Windwalker only just jumped out of the way of a great fifty-foot long Bee-Eater Dragon drifting calmly through the canopy with its gigantic cave of a mouth wide open, like an enormous Basking Shark.

Hiccup tried not to think about another *deeper* noise however, way, way down in the blackness. It was the noise that had given the woods their name, the Woods That Howled, and

Hiccup did not want to think about it, not for a second.

But he knew what it was. It was the Beast...

On through the forest they flew, looking and looking for Fishlegs.

They found nothing but trees, trees and more trees.

And then Hiccup pulled sharply on the reins of the Windwalker as they came upon something unexpected up ahead.

'What *is* that?' whispered Hiccup.

A slight break in the canopy allowed the dappled moonlight to shine through on to a weird shape hovering in the air beside a large honey-tree.

It was a shape absolutely covered from head to

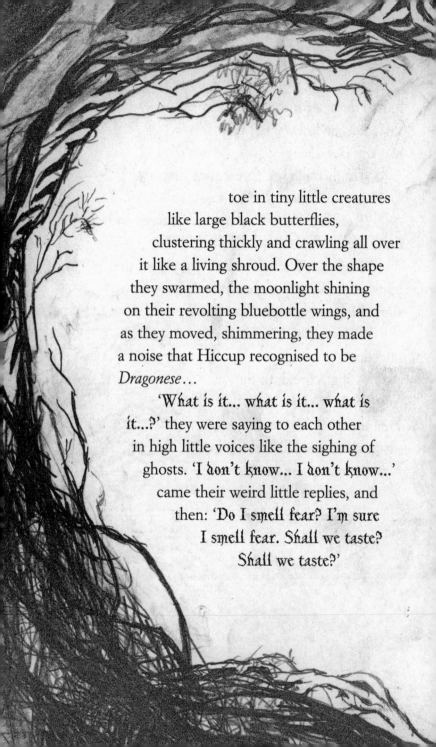

toe in tiny little creatures
like large black butterflies,
clustering thickly and crawling all over
it like a living shroud. Over the shape
they swarmed, the moonlight shining
on their revolting bluebottle wings, and
as they moved, shimmering, they made
a noise that Hiccup recognised to be
Dragonese...

'What is it... what is it... what is
it...?' they were saying to each other
in high little voices like the sighing of
ghosts. 'I don't know... I don't know...'
came their weird little replies, and
then: 'Do I smell fear? I'm sure
I smell fear. Shall we taste?
Shall we taste?'

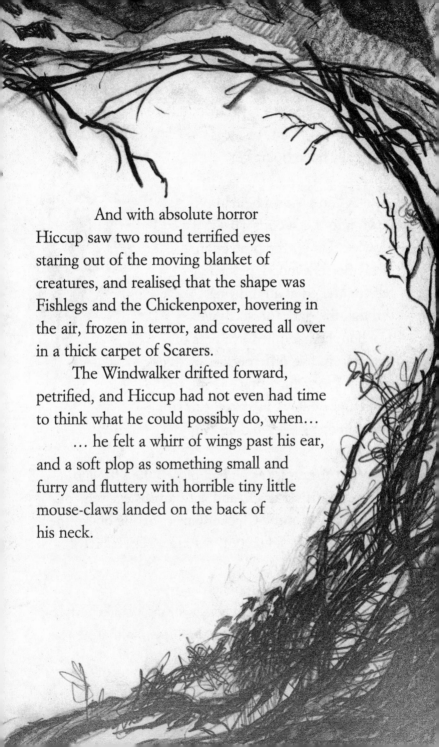

And with absolute horror
Hiccup saw two round terrified eyes
staring out of the moving blanket of
creatures, and realised that the shape was
Fishlegs and the Chickenpoxer, hovering in
the air, frozen in terror, and covered all over
in a thick carpet of Scarers.

The Windwalker drifted forward,
petrified, and Hiccup had not even had time
to think what he could possibly do, when…

… he felt a whirr of wings past his ear,
and a soft plop as something small and
furry and fluttery with horrible tiny little
mouse-claws landed on the back of
his neck.

9. SCARERS

Up until that point, Fishlegs
had really been doing very
well.

All on his own he had
flown into the Woods That
Howled. Under the protection
of his Berserk mood, he hadn't
felt frightened at all of flying
through the dark forest. Brave
as a lion, he had filled five pots of
honey from five different honey trees,
without dropping a single jar on to the
forest floor below. He had been stung
three times by bees and he didn't
even care.

But then, just as he had placed the fifth and
final jar in his rucksack, and with joyous excitement
was about to get the Chickenpoxer soaring out of the
Wood, his heart singing, 'I'm a Hero! I'm a Hero!' –
just at *that* moment…

… something happened.

Who knows what it was, a strange noise perhaps,
a sudden cloud drifting over the moon so that he was

in absolute blackness for a moment. But whatever it was that spooked him caused the sudden disappearance of his Berserk mood as quickly and mysteriously as it had descended upon him.

Fear stole upon Fishlegs as he sat in the heart of that wood, and as soon as he began to get frightened, *that* was when the Scarers came.

Scarers are blind. And a little deaf. But they like to feed upon blood that is filled with the adrenalin caused by fear. And so when a human or an animal is filled with fear, *that* is when they smell them, and gather in thick, cloudy black swarms called 'flutters', tens of thousands strong.

Fishlegs and the Chickenpoxer stayed absolutely still as the Scarers settled upon them. And instinctively they had hit on the right thing to do. For if they stayed still, and calmed their panic, the Scarers might scuttle all over them and then move on, deciding they were a tree, or something else inedible.

Oh for Thor's sake… oh for Thor's sake… what do I do? thought Fishlegs.

And that was when he met Hiccup's eyes, and realised Hiccup was sitting on the hovering Windwalker, only twenty feet or so away.

Fishlegs was always pleased to see Hiccup.

But never in his life had he been more pleased to see him than now.

Hiccup knew all about dragon behaviour. 'What shall I do?' mouthed Fishlegs.

'You're doing the right thing,' hissed Hiccup. 'Don't move a muscle…'

Hiccup and Toothless and the Windwalker also froze. Hiccup could feel the horrible Scarers landing on his neck, on his arms, on his legs, on his chest, on his face, even starting to crawl sluggishly down the back of his collar.

Trembling violently, Fishlegs tried to force himself to stay calm, not to react.

But if YOU have ever been crawled over by spiders, by bats, or by a swarm of angry bees, YOU will know how very very hard it is not to panic. Even if a single *wasp* lands on your arm, it can be hard not to jerk it away instinctively, even though you know that is not the right thing to do.

So just *imagine* how difficult it would be if thousands and thousands of Scarers were swarming all over your body, all over your face even, and maybe they would climb up your nostrils or in your ears…

It was *this* thought that made Fishlegs lose it completely, and who can blame him, frankly.

Scarers!

creepy little bat like ears!!!

spooky little dragon tail!!

~STATISTICS~

COLOURS: Grey/black
ARMED WITH: They suck your BLOOD, enough said
FEAR FACTOR:...................9
ATTACK:.........................7
SPEED:...........................7
SIZE:...............................2
DISOBEDIENCE:...................9

Scarers are spooky little blood-sucking creatures that like to feed on blood filled with adrenalin. Therefore, they scare their prey half to death before they bite them.

'AAAAAIIIIIIIIIIIEEEEEEEEEEE!!!!!!!!!!!!' he screamed, and at exactly the same moment, three Scarers bit the Chickenpoxer on the bottom, and the Chickenpoxer wasn't the kind of dragon to take this lightly. He gave a violent *swish* of his tail, and a maddened buck, and he careered off through the jungle like a fat little Chickenpoxer chunk of lightning, narrowly missing two trees, with Fishlegs screaming wildly and flapping away with his arms on the Chickenpoxer's back.

The Scarers buzzed away in a frenzy and a froth of whirling excitement, before swarming after them in zooming black clouds.

And Fishlegs losing it tipped Hiccup over the edge, and he too started screaming, and the Windwalker bucked in the air before following the others in maddened out-of-control pursuit.

Oh… for… Thor's… sake… thought a terrified Hiccup as he slalomed the Windwalker between the trees. *This is going to end in* DISASTER *just like Fishlegs crashing head-first in the training practice.*

Flying for your life at top speed in the black of the night through the forest of Berserk was a VERY different matter, Hiccup discovered, from that little saunter through the trees in the Almost Wood.

Quite apart from the skill needed to avoid the densely grown trees of the forest, there was the little matter of the swarms of excited Scarers in hot pursuit. Hiccup realised the Scarers were actually shouting out as they followed through the darkness in their weird sing-song scary voices: 'We're going to ge-e-et you...' 'We can see-e-e-e you...'(Not strictly true, because they were blind, but frightening nonetheless.)

That, of course, made the boys and the dragons even *more* scared, and so they gave off even *more* fear hormones, which the pursuing Scarers smelt and that turned them even *more* crazy and drunk and buzzing in a perfect fever of wild hunting excitement, and they swarmed after the boys with a high-pitched screaming whine that woke up *more* Scarers to join in the pursuit, and all in all it was a mad crazy body-chemical-fuelled dragon-chase that zig-zagged and zoomed hysterically through the dark trees of the Woods That Howled that moonlit summer night.

'Thank... you... for... following... me... Hiccup...' yelled Fishlegs as they charged like maniacs through the forest, breaking off twigs and branches and scattering shoals of Squirrelserpents as they went.

'No... problem...' Hiccup shouted back. 'I'm... not... *interfering*... am... I?' he said anxiously as

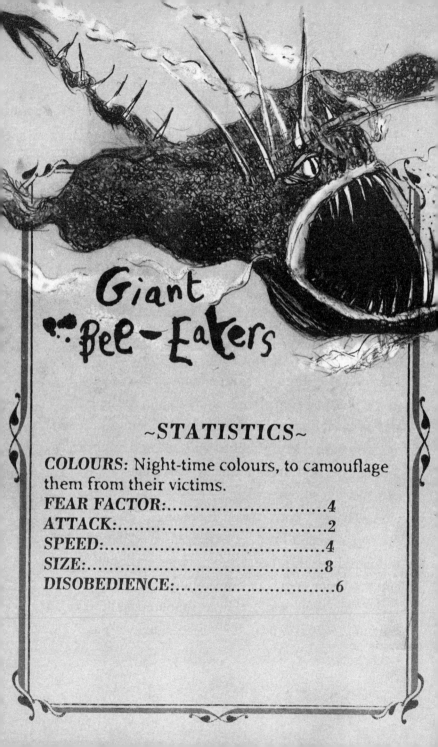

Giant Bee-Eaters

~STATISTICS~

COLOURS: Night-time colours, to camouflage them from their victims.

FEAR FACTOR:..................................4
ATTACK:..2
SPEED:..4
SIZE:...8
DISOBEDIENCE:..............................6

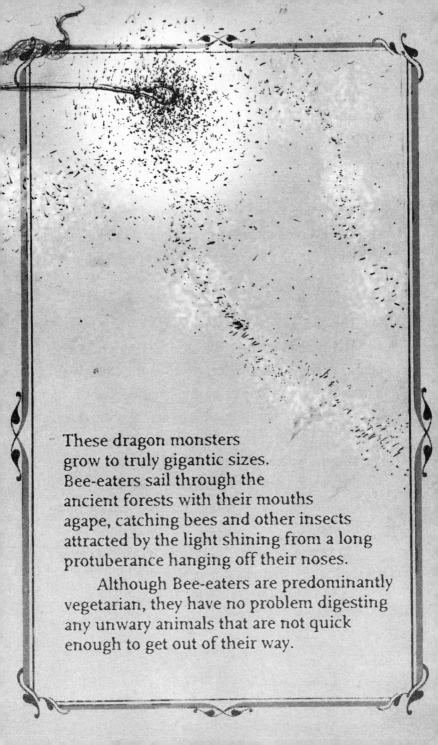

These dragon monsters
grow to truly gigantic sizes.
Bee-eaters sail through the
ancient forests with their mouths
agape, catching bees and other insects
attracted by the light shining from a long
protuberance hanging off their noses.

Although Bee-eaters are predominantly
vegetarian, they have no problem digesting
any unwary animals that are not quick
enough to get out of their way.

he missed a full-on confrontation with a Bee-Eater Dragon by a whisker.

'Of course not,' said Fishlegs, 'you're... OW... HELPING... I was crazy when I said that...'

And then...

This... can't... go... on... much... longer... thought Hiccup as the poor maddened Windwalker's wing-tips swerved violently to the left, skimming the trunk of a tree as they sped like bullets through the tree canopy.

Hiccup was right.

This *couldn't* go on much longer.

The yelling, whining, buzzing chase passed a gigantic sleeping dragon draped up in the treetops, showering it in torn-off twigs and shredded whirls of leaf confetti as it went screaming past, and the dragon opened one eyelid and then another, and then joined the chase in two beats of its languid wings.

And looking over his shoulder, Hiccup saw a great dragon with wings spread out like sails catching up with them.

He barely had time to scream before two more appeared, and there was a strange noise like

Z-I-I-I-I-I-I-I-INNNNNNGGGGG!

And over to his left, a screaming Fishlegs, whose

arms were revolving like whirligigs, lurched wildly as if he had been hit by something, and then slumped over in his saddle as if he were dead. And just as he slumped, the great dark shape of a dragon swooped down and plucked him and the Chickenpoxer out of the air like a hawk pouncing upon a sparrow.

And in the next heartbeat there was another Z-ZI-I-I-I-I-I-I-I-INNNNNNGGGG!

And Hiccup felt a sharp pain in his right shoulder, and that was the last thing he felt before he lost consciousness.

a sharp pain in his right shoulder before he lost consciousness

10. DOES ANYBODY RECOGNISE THIS LOBSTER POT?

'*Helloo-o-o-o-o!* Is there anybody *in* the-e-e-re????'

Somebody is knocking on my helmet... thought Hiccup woozily. *No, that's not possible... I must be dreaming...*

But the knocking continued, like impatient knocking on a metal door, and the banging rang through Hiccup's sleepy brain. *Hang on, I'm coming, don't knock so loudly,* he thought, and he answered the call, opening leaden eyelids...

Somebody was indeed knocking on his helmet.

The Somebody's face was only two inches away from Hiccup's nose, which gave him quite a start. A grinning human Somebody, with a face so heavily tattooed with storms and shipwrecks and trees and giants and serpents that barely a patch of flesh could be seen in between the blue ink.

Hiccup sat up, his head aching with a thumping that now seemed to be knocking from within, and his shoulder tingling with a pins-and-needles numbness.

He was sitting on the floor. Around him in a circle stood huge figures, men and women, vast and muscled, and as crazily tattooed as the man who had been knocking on Hiccup's helmet, and all with great manacles around their wrists, and chains around their legs from which they dragged stones and heavy weights. They were weighed down further by the astonishing amount of weaponry they were carrying, bows and spears and great leaden swords bristling all around them.

BERSERKS, thought Hiccup, and they were indeed.

Fishlegs was lying beside him, similarly trussed up in chains, and he was just waking up. They were lying on a great wooden platform in the centre of what looked like the Berserks' treetop village. Behind them, the Windwalker and the Chickenpoxer were chained to a tree.

The village was the first treetop village Hiccup had ever come across. Every Berserk house had a mast, and a crow's nest, and a rolled-up sail.

The Berserks made their way across the green sea

of the jungle canopy by way of a maze of rope bridges that stretched their way across the entire island, forming a gigantic, fragile web.

From out of one of the largest of the tree-houses, two men came running so swiftly across the rope bridge that Hiccup's heart was in his mouth for fear that the swaying bridge might snap. They were carrying a shield between them, on which there balanced an extraordinary figure, a giant of a man giving a gigantic yawn as he sat bolt upright on the shield, so trussed up with chains and padlocks that he looked for all the world as if he were in a metal straitjacket.

His padlocked arms were bound close about his chest, his legs were chained in a crossed position, his eyes were closed as if in prayer, his back was ramrod straight.

The shield-bearers placed the shield carefully on the wooden platform, and one of the shield-bearers unlocked the many padlocks festooning this extraordinary man. Chain after chain fell down, clattering on to the wooden bridge.

The man still sat there in the legs-crossed position, eyes closed, as if he were a statue. Then, very slowly, he began to uncross his legs, still wound with many ropes of chains but now no longer bound together.

Please ~~turn~~ turn sideways
← to see the Chief Berserk
in all his nutty glory

He got to his feet and planted them firmly apart,
to the gasps and cheers of the watching crowd. Slowly,
slowly, he raised his fists, with the chains still trailing
from them like the wings of some great bird or dragon.

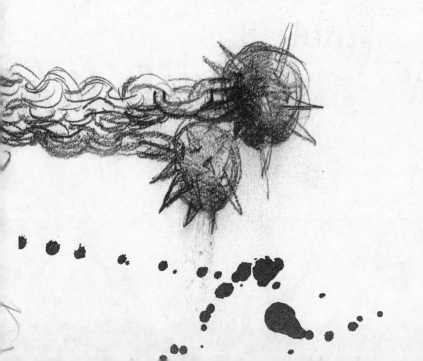

'Hail, Chief! Hail, Chief! Hail, Chief!' roared the crowds.

'O, the Magnificence of ME!!!' yelled the mighty Chieftain.

'O, the Magnificence of YOU!!!' screamed the crowds right back at him.

O, *the* BARMINESS *of the lot of you*, thought Hiccup, his heart sinking as he realised that this lot had more than the usual Archipelago loopiness about them.

Hiccup remembered that the Berserks chained themselves up in order to restrain their Berserkness. They did everything in their chains: practised sword-fighting, everything – and then when they fought in battle, they

He's BERSERK! He's BERSERK!

threw off their chains and went BERSERK.*

The Chief Berserk scooped up a handful of
Electrisquirms who were innocently chomping through
some leaves on the branch above him, and held them
tight in his clenched fist.

Immediately his body quivered with electricity.
Of course, he was covered from head to toe in metal
chains so the electric shocks must have been far worse
for him. But he stood there, red in the face like a
tomato with the flu, his body quivering and jerking as
the electricity coursed through him, with the crowd
cheering, 'HE'S BERSERK! HE'S BERSERK! HE'S
A NUTTER, WATCH HIM JERK!'

Hmmm, thought Hiccup. That *can't be good for
your mental state…* as the sparks flew off the Chief

---

* Athletes do something similar when they are training for
the Olympics.

a NUTTER! Watch him JERK!!

Berserk's horns and his moustache began to smoke.

'WHO'S THE MAN?' roared the Chief Berserk, finally releasing the Electrisquirms and throwing them into the crowd.

'YOU'RE THE MAN!' yelled the happy crowds back at him.

'AM I A NUTTER?' bellowed the Chief Berserk.

'YOU CERTAINLY ARE!' clapped the crowds with joyful acclamation.

'AM I NOT MAGNIFICENT? AM I NOT MARVELLOUS? AM I NOT THE SPLENDIDEST? LOOK ON MY SWORD O MIGHTY ONES AND DESPAIR!'

The Chief Berserk stood there, acknowledging the applause, with his muscles flexed and his sword raised above his head. Unfortunately the dignity of the moment was slightly ruined by Toothless, who had flapped groggily out of Hiccup's basket and happened to be hovering slightly above the Chief Beserk's head at the time. Toothless's magnetised stomach was instantly attracted to the metal of the Chief Berserk's sword, and ended up stuck to it (luckily to the flat side of the blade rather than the point).

The Chief Berserk blinked in surprise.

You don't really expect a small green dragon to appear out of nowhere and inexplicably stick to your sword. The Chief Berserk shook the sword. The little dragon's tummy remained jammed flat to the blade. In disbelief, the Chief Berserk shook the sword from side to side as hard as he could. Toothless squeaked in protest, but he did not budge.

'Sabotage!' roared the Berserk. 'GERRIMOFF!'

Hiccup stepped forward politely. 'Erm, Your Loopiness,' he said, 'allow me...'

Hiccup pulled Toothless off the sword. The little dragon immediately stuck to the Berserk's head.

'I apologise for my dragon, Your Loopiness...' said Hiccup, pulling Toothless off the Berserk's helmet, only for him to immediately stick fast to the Berserk's breast-plate. 'He's... er... a *magic* dragon, you see...' As Hiccup suspected, the superstitious crowd reacted with wonder. 'OOOH...' they chorused, 'a *magic* dragon...'

Hiccup finally removed Toothless from the Berserk's breastplate, only for the little dragon to stick BOING on to the Berserk's chained ankle, from where Hiccup wrestled him off and put him carefully down his waistcoat again.

'SHUDDUP!' roared the Chief Berserk. 'Magic

12₃

my bottom! I'm the only one here with magical powers! And why have my slumbers been disturbed on this Night of the Full Moon?'

'More victims, Your Barminess,' said the Berserk-Who-Had-Knocked, bowing low. 'The Poison Darters just brought them in.'

In the treetops a little way away, four great dragons were making the trees sway madly as they devoured a meal of something bloody and nameless. The Berserks must have trained the Poison Darters to bring in their victims for them.

'Fiancés, by the look of them,' said another Berserk, who had peered inside Fishlegs's rucksack.

'They're awfully *small*, for Fiancés,' sniffed the Chief Berserk. 'And UG sent a message to say not to expect any more Fiancés till after the Full Moon.'

'Yes, but they've got the honey and everything,' said the Berserk-Who-Had-Knocked.

'YOU!' yelled the Chief Berserk. 'Boy with the red hair! Are you really a Fiancé of Princess Tantrum O'UGerly?'

'What happens if I'm not?' answered Hiccup cautiously.

'Well if you're *not* a Fiancé of Tantrum O'UGerly, *or* a political enemy of UG the Uglithug, you're not

124

good enough for the Dead-of-Night Ceremony and we just tip you over the bridge,' replied the Chief Berserk, pointing to the dizzying depths below the platform.

'In which case we are most definitely Fiancés,' said Hiccup firmly. 'What is the Dead-of-Night Ceremony?'

'That's the Ceremony where we feed the Fiancés to the Beast,' explained the Chief Berserk.

Oh great. Maybe being tipped over the bridge would have been better.

'ALPHONSE!' yelled the Chief Berserk.

Across one of the rope bridges a hooded man came limping. Numerous cooking implements were hanging from his belt... forks, wooden spoons, knives, enormous whisks, machetes and axes for hacking meat carcasses apart, all clanging into each other so that he clanked as he walked like a man made out of metal.

'Alphonse is my Talented-but-Emotional French Chef,' boasted the Chief Berserk, in an aside to Hiccup. 'We eat very well here on Berserk, you know. We're not TOTAL barbarians.'

'I'm sure you're not,' said Hiccup tactfully.

The Chef limped forward, clank, clang, clank. His brown cloak was so long that it swept the wooden floor, and his hood drooped in a shroud across his face as if he were the figure of Death Himself.

'Alphonse,' queried the Chief Berserk. 'I want your opinion as a Top French Chef. Do you think we should fatten these Fiancés up a bit, and feed them to the Beast at the *next* Full Moon? They look a little skinny to provide the Beast with a proper juicy meal.'

The Chef responded in a strong but unconvincing French accent. He sounded amused. 'Non, non, non,' he tutted. 'A few 'erbs, a few spices and zey will be just as good as ze others. *Better* per'aps. We 'ave a saying back in France. "Ze smaller zey are, ze *sweeter* zey are."

Alphonse the Talented-but-Emotion French Chef seems strangely FAMILIAR...

clank
clank

And I 'ave a feeling zat zese liddle ones will be ve-e-e-e-e-ery sweet indeed.'

His voice was strangely familiar.

Hiccup tried to peer under the hood, but it drooped so low it was impossible to see his face.

'Your accent is terrible,' said Hiccup suspiciously to the Chef, in impeccable French. Hiccup was very good at languages.

'It isn't half as bad as my cooking,' replied the man in the hood, in much less good French, and with an ironical bow.

'Thank you, Alphonse,' said the Chief Berserk, waving him away with a regal hand. 'OK! Chain up these latest Fiancés, and put them in their cages, and let's all go back to bed. Only three more hours and we've got to be up for the Dead-of-Night Ceremony. We need to be rested to do all that howling.'

Fishlegs had been trying to work up the nerve to say something for the past couple of minutes.

'Erm… excuse me…' he said.

Hmm…

I am
= a
BERSERK !

The Chief
Berserk
turned to

The Chief of Berserk
is FLABBERGASTED

him with an eyebrow raised
in surprise. 'Don't tell me, you've got a very good
reason why you can't participate in the Ceremony
tonight,' he said. 'I've heard every single excuse in
the book from you Fiancés. "My pimples make me
poisonous," "I'm missing a very important dentist
appointment," "I've got a note from my mother saying
I can't be fed to the Beast today..." I've heard 'em
all... What's *your* excuse, then?'

Fishlegs stood up and said boldly, sticking out
his chest, 'We aren't the Supper. We can't be. Because
I...' Fishlegs swallowed hard, and pointed to his heart,
'... *I*... am a Berserk.'

It came out slightly quieter than Fishlegs had
imagined it. But it was still a good moment. Fishlegs,
standing tall and illuminated in a pool of moonlight

in the middle of a circle of gratifyingly astonished Berserks.

'*You*... are a Berserk???' repeated the Chief Berserk, jabbing a muscly forefinger at Fishlegs.

'That's right,' said Fishlegs. 'I'm a Berserk who has been brought up by Hooligans. We only really realised it when I started showing Berserk tendencies a year or so ago, or I'd have come earlier. But thirteen years ago when I was a baby, I drifted into the Harbour at Berk inside this very lobster pot...'

Fishlegs took the lobster pot off his shoulders to show them.

'That isn't a lobster pot,' the Chief Berserk pointed out. 'It's a rucksack.'

'It's a lobster pot that I have **MADE** into a rucksack,' explained Fishlegs. 'And I was wondering, you know, if any of you might recognise this particular lobster pot? Or... you know... remember if thirteen years ago, one of you, maybe, accidentally dropped a *baby* in this particular lobster pot? Which then drifted out to sea in a sort of westerly direction...' Fishlegs swallowed. This was harder to explain than he had thought, in front of a circle of flabbergasted Berserk eyes. 'And I was thinking,' stammered Fishlegs, 'that, perhaps, under the circumstances... you might forget about the Feeding-us-to-the-Beast-in-the-Spooky-Ceremony business? On account of… on account of… on account of… I'm *family*.'

Silence for a moment.

Oh please, thought Hiccup, *please, feed us to the Beast if you must, but please please please just let him down gently.*

HA! HA! HA! HA! HA! HA

More silence, and then…

'FAMILY???' splutted the Chief Berserk.
'Family???? HA HA HA HA HA HA HA!'

'HA HA HA HA HA HA HA!!!' roared
the Berserks, merrily shaking their chains in their
amusement.

The Chief Berserk wiped the tears from his eyes
with one tattooed hand. 'Oh, Boy with a Face like a
Haddock that Somebody Trod on,' laughed the Chief
Berserk. '*We* are not your family. Look at you, you've
got arms like pieces of seaweed! No, if *we* were indeed
the ones who put you in that lobster pot thirteen years
ago, well there would have been no *accident* about it.
We have a little tradition here in the Berserk Tribe.
We give our babies to the Naming Dame directly after
the birth, and if they're a little weak, a little sickly, a
little weird, like *you* are, well, SHE gives them the
name of a RUNT, and WE leave them on a handy
mountainside, or cast them out to sea in something
floaty, and let Thor take care of them.'

'Ah,' said Fishlegs.

'*Toss out the freak, or the Tribe will be weak,*'
grinned the Chief Berserk. 'That's an old saying of
us Berserks. But it needn't have been *us*, you know,

A! HA! HA! HA! HA!

it could have been *any one* of the
Archipelago Tribes, we all have the same
tradition, Hooligans included. I'm surprised you
haven't heard of it.'

'No,' said Fishlegs
gloomily,
'but
now you
come to
mention
it, the
Hooligans
do have a
similar saying,
*Only the strong
can belong*.'

YOU
are a
BERSERK?

'Tell you
what, though,' said
the Chief Berserk,
still chortling and holding
his sides, 'you've given me
such a laugh, I'll let you be a Fiancé
anyway, despite being such a runt.'

Fishlegs stood looking at his lobster pot for
a moment.

He pushed his glasses up his nose.

And then he put the lobster pot back on his shoulders again.

'I guess…' said Fishlegs slowly, and very very tiredly, 'I guess that's what I should have expected. I just *hoped*…' He let the sentence trail off.

'Get these boys chained up here! And let's all have some kip, I'm knackered!' yelled the Chief Berserk. '*Family!!!!*' He shook his head. 'That's the best excuse I've ever heard. Oh, these Fiancés, they'll be the death of me, they really will… Well, I must say that makes an excellent bag of Fiancés for the Ceremony tonight. I make that *thirteen* Fiancés in all… lucky I'm not superstitious…'

'Just one more thing, Your Loopiness,' said Hiccup. 'You haven't got my friend Camicazi the Bog-Burglar captured anywhere around here, have you?'

The Chief Berserk looked at Hiccup thoughtfully. 'By Camicazi, do you mean a little girl with blonde hair who bites?'

'That's the one,' said Hiccup.

'Never heard of her,' said the Chief Berserk.

The Fiancés were being kept in cages on the outskirts of the village.

The boys were wrapped round and around in chains until they resembled little metal mummies, and rolled into two empty cages at the end of the row. And then the Berserks stretched their tattooed arms above their heads and yawned, and went back to bed, to rest up their tonsils for the excitements of the Dead-of-Night Ceremony in only four hours' time.

I guess that's what I should have expected. I just hoped....

11. THE FIANCÉ-BEFORE-THE FIANCÉ-BEFORE-LAST

'I'm sorry, Fishlegs,' whispered Hiccup, from the darkness of the cage suspended way way way above the forest floor.

'Oh, don't worry,' sighed Fishlegs, his voice still tight with disappointment. 'I wouldn't exactly be thrilled to find that I was related to these guys anyway. Even by Archipelago standards they seem more than extraordinarily loopy. It's just that it would be nice, just once, to be the Hero and not the Big Joke. And it would be nice to know who my family were.'

'*We're* your family, us Hooligans,' whispered Hiccup. 'Toothless and me. In the meantime.'

There was another long pause.

'Thanks for following me, Hiccup,' Fishlegs whispered back after some time.

'Excuse me,' said a voice from the cage next door, the moonlight illuminating a young man wearing a helmet with the distinctive horns of the Lost Tribe. 'Sorry to disturb, but the guy two cages down would like to have a word with you.'

'HICCUP!' bellowed a hearty voice from three

cages down. 'HICCUP HORRENDOUS HADDOCK
THE THIRD! I COULDN'T REALLY SEE WHO
YOU WERE WITH ALL THOSE BERSERKS
ROUND YOU, BUT FANCY MEETING YOU
HERE!'

'Who's that?' whispered Hiccup, trying to
squint through the cages and the darkness, and seeing
nothing but the dim outline of someone bobbing up
and down with excitement.

'It's *me*!' bellowed the voice. 'Humungously
Hotshot the Hero! Don't you remember? Lava-Lout
island? The thousands and thousands of Exterminator
Dragons? The volcano exploding?* Now that was a
tight spot…'

A ripple of excitement went along the cages.

1st Fiancé: 'I don't believe it! It's Humungously
Hotshot the Hero!'

5th Fiancé: 'It's almost *worth* being fed horribly
to the Beast, just to have the pleasure of meeting the
bravest, coolest man in the Archipelago…'

8th Fiancé: 'NONSENSE! I am in fact the
bravest, coolest man in the Archipelago, and I notice
that this Hotshot has lost some weight. A proper Hero
has a good proper belly…'

5th Fiancé: 'How *dare* you say that about

---

* You can read about this in *How to Twist a Dragon's Tale*.

Humungously Hotshot the Hero! Reach for your
sword and meet me with steel!'

8th Fiancé: (promptly) 'Whenever and
Wheresoever you wish!'

5th Fiancé: (between gritted teeth) 'Your face, is
uglier than a baboon's bottom…'

8th Fiancé: 'And *you* have the mug of a pig with
the plague…'

5th Fiancé: 'FOOL!'

8th Fiancé: 'MORON!'

5th Fiancé: 'VEGETARIAN!'

And if only they had been free, the Fiancés would clearly have been swordfighting madly, but as it was they were heavily chained and trussed up, so all they could do was throw themselves wildly

about their cages, which they did with gusto.

'Ignore them,' grinned Humungous, 'they do that all day long. What are *you* doing here, Hiccup?'

'I seem to be Princess Tantrum's twelfth Fiancé. And how about YOU?' asked Hiccup, immensely cheered by the presence of Humungous, whom he admired enormously. 'I thought you would Never Love Again?'

Humungous's *last* Impossible Task had led to him spending fifteen years in the Lava-Lout Jail Forges, which was enough to put anybody off.

'Oh, that was before I met HER,' said Humungous rapturously, and he shook a Heroic fist at the moon above. 'CAN'T A MAN HAVE A SECOND CHANCE?' he shouted at the starry heavens.

1st Fiancé: 'YOU BETCHA!'
3rd Fiancé: 'TOO RIGHT…'
5th Fiancé: 'YESSIREE!'

The Fiancés rattled their cages madly.

'IT IS AN HONOUR TO DIE FOR THE LOVE OF PRINCESS TANTRUM!' cried Humungous, Heroic to the last. And now the you betchas and the yessirees were a little more thoughtful from the other Fiancés, as if they hadn't

140

bargained on actually *dying* for their love.

'But dying is out of the question!' called out Humungously Hotshot. 'Princess Tantrum would be so *upset*. We must get out of here at all costs.'

'Easier said than done. And even if by some miracle we were to get out of here, who is she going to marry?' Hiccup pointed out.

All the Fiancés together: 'ME!'

'Well she can't marry *all* of you,' Hiccup said. 'Hang on a second... How many cages away are you, Humungous? One, two, three... HUMUNGOUS! *You* must be the Fiancé-Before-the-Fiancé-Before-Last! Congratulations!'

'I suppose I must,' admitted Humungously Hotshot. 'And thank you. What does that mean?'

'Princess Tantrum said the Fiancé she was in LOVE with was the Fiancé-Before-the-Fiancé-Before-Last,' explained Hiccup.

Humungous coughed modestly. 'I suspected she might be,' he said.

1st Fiancé: 'Well, *that's* a bit of a blow.'

6th Fiancé: 'You mean... considering we're all about to be fed to the Beast and everything?'

3rd Fiancé: 'Yes, I think it's pretty gutting really... I spent a lot of *time* on that love poetry, I really did, it was soppy as anything.'

4th Fiancé: 'Oh, did you write it yourself? I got mine from a little bard I know down in the Weird Territories. I'll give you directions if you like, in case we get out of here and you want to use him for next time.'

3rd Fiancé: 'You know though, to be frank with you, I've been wondering whether for me there will actually BE a next time? I mean, is this whole LOVE thing really worth it? It's too *dangerous*.'

2nd Fiancé: 'Yes I *know*, and did you see the FATHER-IN-LAW? Put me off a bit, I can tell you... I'm not sure I fancy popping over THERE for family get-togethers, ho-ho...'

All the Fiancés together: 'You betcha!... *Too* right!... YESIREEE!'

'But this is marvellous!' cried Humungously Hotshot the Hero. 'NOW all we need to do is to think of a way out of here, and it's happy endings all round! Unfortunately I'm a little tied up here. I've been trying to bite my way out, but I haven't had a lot of luck.'

'The chains are metal,' explained Hiccup.

'But *you'll* come up with a Plan, Hiccup,' said Humungously Hotshot, with touching confidence. 'You're a brainy chap. Quiet now, everyone. Hiccup is thinking, and we haven't got much time.'

Toothless snored loudly inside Hiccup's
waistcoat, groaning and holding his tummy. At any
other time Hiccup would be worried to death about
him, but right now he had too much else to be
thinking of. Quietness descended on the thirteen
cages, swinging gently up in the treetops. Hiccup
thought and he thought, but no Plan came to him.

And as Hiccup thought, one by one the Fiancés
fell asleep, until only Fishlegs was awake. Fishlegs's
cage was so beset by Scarers that you could barely see
poor Fishlegs within it.

'I WISH I was as stupid as those Fiancés,' sighed
Fishlegs. 'And then I wouldn't have to be scared the
whole time.'

The Fiancés were indeed snoring without a care
in the world, as if they were snoozing on grassy knolls
safe on their cosy island homes, rather than facing
death by sacrifice in only a couple of hours.

It *did* seem a little unfair.

But such was the gentle rocking of the cages, and
the snoring of the Fiancés, and the humming, buzzing,
droning of the Berserk bees in the background, that
eventually even Fishlegs and Hiccup dozed off too,
Hiccup's dreaming mind full of impossible escapes.

And Hiccup had only just dropped off before he was woken, this time by a noise. In the pitchy blackness, there was the sound of footsteps walking along the wooden bridge towards him. Or, to be more precise, the sound of one footstep followed by a tap... the tap of someone, say, who had a wooden leg... and who was dragging chains behind him.

Step...tap...clank clank...step...tap...clank clank...step...tap...step...tap...step...tap...clank clank.

Hiccup cringed back as far as he could into the cage... but of course, there was nowhere to go.

And slowly into the cage there reached...

... a terrible black hook, which caught Hiccup by the collar and dragged him up to the bars, where he came face to face with the one eye, and the wooden nose, and the glittering evil smile...

Of...

Blistering Whiskers and Anchovy Armpits and Great Hairy Toenails of Thor!

Hiccup hardly dared to think that this adventure could get even WORSE.

But it looked horribly like it might be Alvin the Treacherous.

12. ALPHONSE THE TALENTED-BUT-EMOTIONAL FRENCH CHEF

Alvin the Treacherous was Hiccup's arch-enemy.

The last time Hiccup met him he thought he really HAD got rid of him, for in front of Hiccup's eyes Alvin had been swallowed by a Fire-Dragon that then dived down into a volcano. How could *even* Alvin have escaped from the fiery waters of the Earth's core?

But, then again, there were things about Alvin that made him easy to recognise.

One eye covered by a black eye patch, the other glinting with evil. One leg stamping and muscly, the other capped at the knee with an ivory stump. The moonlight bouncing off his paper-white skull.

These are the kind of features that you don't really forget about a person, even if you haven't seen them in quite a while.

The only difference was that Alvin used to have a large and arrogant nose.

This man had no nose at all.

Which is never a good look.

He had fashioned himself a nose out of wood,

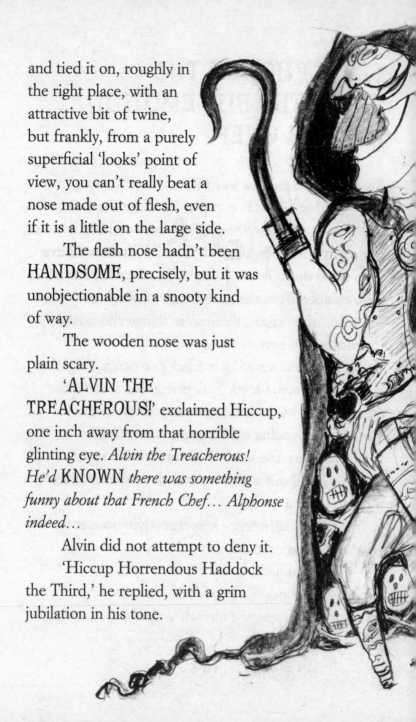

and tied it on, roughly in the right place, with an attractive bit of twine, but frankly, from a purely superficial 'looks' point of view, you can't really beat a nose made out of flesh, even if it is a little on the large side.

The flesh nose hadn't been HANDSOME, precisely, but it was unobjectionable in a snooty kind of way.

The wooden nose was just plain scary.

'ALVIN THE TREACHEROUS!' exclaimed Hiccup, one inch away from that horrible glinting eye. *Alvin the Treacherous! He'd* KNOWN *there was something funny about that French Chef... Alphonse indeed...*

Alvin did not attempt to deny it.

'Hiccup Horrendous Haddock the Third,' he replied, with a grim jubilation in his tone.

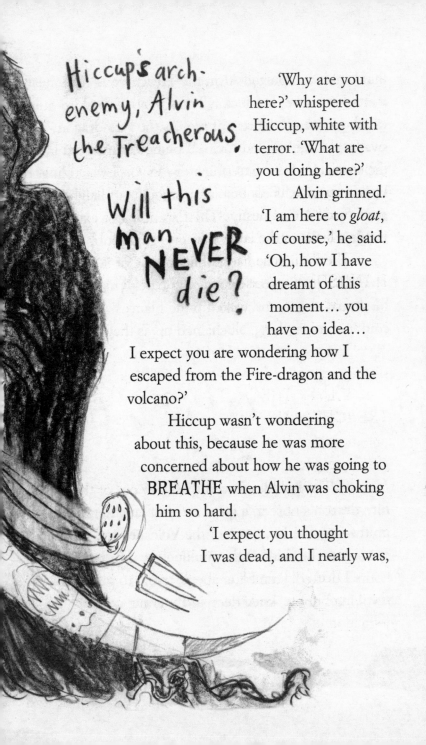

Hiccup's arch-enemy, Alvin the Treacherous.

Will this man NEVER die?

'Why are you here?' whispered Hiccup, white with terror. 'What are you doing here?'

Alvin grinned. 'I am here to *gloat*, of course,' he said. 'Oh, how I have dreamt of this moment… you have no idea… I expect you are wondering how I escaped from the Fire-dragon and the volcano?'

Hiccup wasn't wondering about this, because he was more concerned about how he was going to **BREATHE** when Alvin was choking him so hard.

'I expect you thought I was dead, and I nearly was,

thanks to *you*,' purred Alvin the Treacherous. 'The heat melted my nose, but luckily I was wearing my Fire-Suit, which protected the rest of me. As the Fire-dragon swallowed me,' smiled Alvin, 'I plunged my sword into the stomach of the Exterminator Dragon I was riding. Dragon stomachs contain large amounts of laughing gas…' said Alvin craftily. 'The Exterminator exploded inside the Fire-dragon's throat into great bubbles of gas, one of which had *me* in the middle of it.'

Hiccup's scared brain could barely think. Perhaps he should shout, and wake up the Fiancés? But *they* couldn't do anything, all chained up as they were.

'The bubbles forced their way out of the Fire-dragon's nose in a great snort of laughter, and rose up through the Lava, out of the Volcano, and floated out across the skies of the Archipelago. For hours and hours I drifted, stumbling about, trying to burst that revolting bubble, knee-deep in Exterminator

stomach contents, and laughing manically from the laughing gas...'

'YUCKY...' groaned Hiccup.

'Quite so,' said Alvin. 'Until I happened by chance to drift over the island of Berserk, and my bubble was shot down by a Berserk arrow. I fell from the sky like a stone, landing on the head of Berserk's Chief Chef, and killing him outright. Chief Berserk explained he was going to slaughter me as a punishment' – (Alvin's teeth smiled on, but he had the watchful look of a cobra about to strike in his one good eye, and Hiccup kept on looking at that hook) – 'so I told him that I, too, was a Chef. He believed me, the fool, and I have been cooking for him ever since, three meals a day, may his toes turn to coral. But it was worth it, Hiccup... all worth it for this moment... Here you are, imprisoned in a cage, alone and afraid, facing a terrible death... and I am going to kill you now, Death by Hook!'

Alvin threw back his head to laugh.

Hiccup's heart was beating as quick and fast as the heart of a bird caught in the paws of a malevolent fox, and his hands were clammy with sweat. But he forced himself to speak calmly and politely.

'I'm not sure that I would say that you were "free as a bird", Alvin...'

Alvin stopped mid-laugh, and turned his glittering eye to Hiccup. 'What do you mean?' he said through gritted teeth. 'This better be good, you're spoiling my moment...'

'*Well, look at you,*' Hiccup pointed out. 'You're in chains, like I am. Instead of *gloating* over me, why don't you get me to help you to *escape*?'

Alvin paused.

'You have a plan to escape???' said Alvin, in disbelief.

'Of course I have,' said Hiccup as carelessly as he could. (This wasn't strictly true, but Hiccup was sure that something would come to him eventually.) 'You've seen me escape before, haven't you, right in front of everybody's eyes in that packed amphitheatre in Fort Sinister? This is going to be pretty much the same sort of situation, I'd say...' Hiccup tried to sound casual. 'In fact it should be easy-peasy in comparison...'

'Easy-peasy...' repeated Alvin in a sort of glazed way.*

Alvin had been imagining this moment for so long, going over every detail, of how Hiccup would sob, and call for his mother, and beg for mercy, and tell Alvin how evil and clever Alvin had been.

And here Hiccup was, looking supremely relaxed and talking about escaping...

---

* He remembered that escape from Fort Sinister with bitter fury. He certainly didn't want that happening again, and Hiccup slipping through his hook right at the last moment.

It was profoundly irritating.

'Of course,' said Alvin, cheering up, 'I could take the element of chance out of it by going ahead and killing you RIGHT NOW...' Alvin's good hand crept towards his sword.

'But then I wouldn't be able to help you to escape,' said Hiccup hurriedly. 'And you can always kill me AFTER we get away...' he added soothingly.

Alvin looked at Hiccup for a long, long time, thinking hard. And then he withdrew his hook from the cage.

Hiccup let out a tiny, inward breath of relief.

A reprieve... *for the moment*.

Alvin had controlled his anger.

Two could play at this game... so when Alvin next spoke, he was as polite as Hiccup, if not more so. And with a charming smile with far too many teeth in it, he said:

'You're right, maybe Death by Hook IS too quick and easy a way for you to go. So, what's your plan for escaping then?'

'First,' said Hiccup, 'you get me out of this cage. Second, you take me to where Camicazi is imprisoned...'

Alvin gave a start of surprise – so Hiccup was

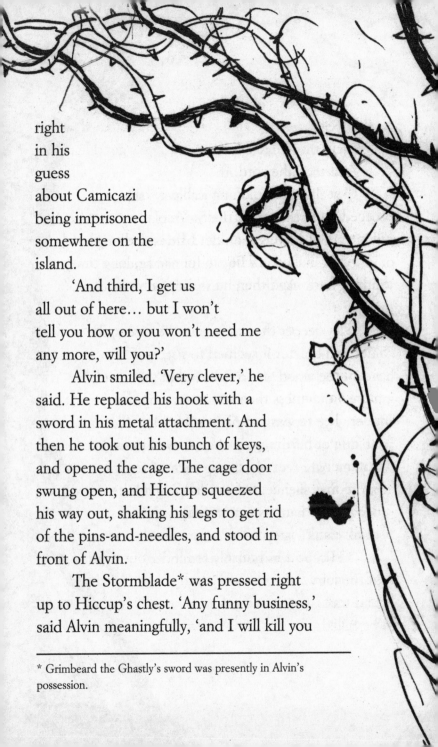

right
in his
guess
about Camicazi
being imprisoned
somewhere on the
island.

'And third, I get us
all out of here… but I won't
tell you how or you won't need me
any more, will you?'

Alvin smiled. 'Very clever,' he
said. He replaced his hook with a
sword in his metal attachment. And
then he took out his bunch of keys,
and opened the cage. The cage door
swung open, and Hiccup squeezed
his way out, shaking his legs to get rid
of the pins-and-needles, and stood in
front of Alvin.

The Stormblade* was pressed right
up to Hiccup's chest. 'Any funny business,'
said Alvin meaningfully, 'and I will kill you

---

* Grimbeard the Ghastly's sword was presently in Alvin's
possession.

on the spot.'

Alvin thrust Hiccup forward.

And then they set off.

Out along the shaking walkways they proceeded, Hiccup first, the Stormblade pricking between his shoulder blades, walking on the spider's web of fragile human bridges, winding their way through the tangled mass of the forest.

The deeper they went into the forest, the colder and quieter it seemed to get, as if the heart of the wood was dead. And in that dead, inhuman quietness their footsteps rang out the louder. The tapping of Alvin's ivory leg, the clanking of his dragging chains, even the soft shaking bare feet of Hiccup seemed to ring out in that silence. He was limping a little because he had a splinter. Step…tap… clank clank…step…tap…clank clank…

Hiccup was horribly reminded of the fairy story in which the child was taken into the forest to be killed.

He could feel poor floppy, feverish Toothless stirring in his waistcoat. The little dragon's hot breath was so faint now that it was barely there. The frantic pace of the last couple of hours had meant that Hiccup hadn't been concentrating on Toothless's illness, which suddenly seemed to have got much worse. Now Hiccup had a terrible instinct that the little dragon was going downhill so fast he was very close to death.

Maybe Fate meant them both to die here together, in the heart of the wood.

Eventually, Alvin stopped in front of one particularly large tree.

'Here we are,' he said.

Hiccup swallowed. 'What is this?' he asked. This time, his voice really *did* shake a little, even though he tried to control it.

Dark, strangling ivy clustered thick about the trunk of the giant tree. With a graceful flick of the Stormblade, Alvin swept the thick fronds away like

curtains, and there, cut into the trunk and right
through to the hollow core of the tree... was a little
door of metal bars. Alvin opened it. Inside was a trap-
door, which Alvin pulled up.

'So this is where Camicazi is being held, is it?'
said Hiccup.

'That's right,' said Alvin again, a truly nasty smile
on his face. 'Inside this tree. So, in you hop then... the
rescuing Hero. What are you waiting for?'

The Stormblade was pointing at his chest. What
choice did he have?

Slowly, reluctantly, Hiccup clambered through
the trap-door and into the tree.

There was a rope ladder hanging down on the
inside, and he perched there.

As soon as he had done so, Alvin slammed
the door shut, and thrust his hand through the bars,
grabbing Hiccup by the shirt front again,
just as he had done in the cage, only this
time with his hand rather than his
hook.

'And NOW, Mister
Hiccup, NOW I can
truly gloat! You will die
here nice and slowly

in the dark, for NO ONE has ever made their way out of one of these living, growing prison cells.'

Hiccup looked down quickly, and Alvin only smiled the wider.

'And no,' he said, 'this is not Camicazi's cell. I have no idea who is down there. But I think they are alive, for we generally know they are dead from the SMELL.'

Alvin began to hack away at the ropes of the ladder, and Hiccup half climbed, half fell down the inside of the tree, landing on the hollowed-out bottom of the prison-cell, on what felt like pine-needles, twisting his body so that he didn't land on Toothless.

'REVENGE IS SWEET!!!!' were the last words that Alvin shouted down to him in the blackness, and the words reverberated around the inside of the trunk of the tree, as did the sound of the door clanging shut again and the key being turned in the lock.

And as Hiccup lay in the utter utter darkness, he realised, from a slight rustling sound to his left, that he was not alone.

13. IN THE DARK

There it was again, the sound.

With trembling fingers, Hiccup drew his sword.

It shook in his hand.

'HELLO?' said Hiccup, his words sounding very loud in that darkness.

Silence.

Hiccup had never known a darkness like it. It was so thick about him that it choked the throat and clogged the nostrils and stuffed the ears like a smothering cloak.

And it came with a sense, an instinct that Hiccup couldn't put his finger on, that he was sharing the tree with something overpoweringly evil.

Another rustling
noise, and to Hiccup's
petrified imagination it seemed
like something might be moving
towards him, and so he shouted
wildly, 'I HAVE A SWORD!'

The rustling stopped abruptly.

And then a voice in the darkness
came hissing like a serpent at Hiccup.

'And *so*,' said the voice, 'do *I*...'

'I'M NOT AFRAID OF YOU!'
announced Hiccup, as loud as he
could to give himself confidence.

'Ohhh, yes you *are*,' spat
the voice. 'And you are right
to be.'

An old voice,
a female voice,
a voice with

an icy edge of
purest evil to it.

Hiccup lay quaking in the
dark, his left hand holding his sword,
his right protecting the limp little body
of Toothless.

'Who are you?' hissed the voice.
'And why didn't I see you coming?'

'How could you see me coming?'
stammered Hiccup. 'You are in the
dark.'

'I am a witch,' said the voice.

Ohhhhhhhhhhh great.

'Who are you?' repeated
the voice.

Hiccup thought fast. For some
reason he didn't want to tell her his
real name.

'My name is Fishlegs.' Which
was the first name that came into
his head. 'Who are you?'

'My name is Hogtrude,' replied the witch.

(Hiccup had a feeling that wasn't *her* real name either.)

'Why are you here?' asked the witch.

'I was sent here by UG,' replied Hiccup.

'UG normally comes himself, and alone. Why did he send *you*?' spat the voice.

Toothless's floppy body hung heavy in Hiccup's hand. In a stroke of pure inspiration Hiccup thought, *Well if she's a witch* maybe she can help Toothless.*

---

* A 'witch' or a 'wizard' at that time was wise in the use of herbs, medicines and potions. They acted as 'witch doctors' to the Tribes, as well as looking into the future.

'I am bringing a dragon for you to heal,' he said.

Silence again.

'Where is the dragon?' hissed the voice.

Hiccup held Toothless up, and bony fingers came creeping out of the darkness, and felt Toothless's little limp, moaning, drooping body.

'HA!' snapped the voice. 'Does UG think I'm a miracle worker? This dragon is as good as dead already.'

'Isn't there ANYTHING you can do?' asked Hiccup desperately. 'UG is very very fond of this dragon, and he said he would give you anything you needed, anything at all...'

'Herbs, poisons, needles-and-thread,' creaked the voice, muttering resentful noises to itself. 'He'll give me these but he won't give me my freedom...

Oh I'm

telling you, when
UG comes here to ask for
his Fortune, I tell him pretty lies
but if UG only knew what a Fortune
I was weaving him…'

Shivering at the sheer savagery of the
voice's tone, Hiccup kept silent. He cradled
Toothless in his arms, stroking his ears and
horns, and trying to keep him comfortable.
Toothless had lost so much weight that he
was a little bag of bones, but his belly was
horribly swollen and distended.

'What's wrong with the dying
dragon?' asked the voice, when it had
finished its muttering.

'He ate a spoon,' said Hiccup,
'and a magic stone… and other
things I expect.'

'A spoon…' repeated
the voice longingly.

The witch
didn't have a
spoon.

And though it may not seem like much of a treasure, when you've spent twenty years trying to eat soup with a *fork*, a spoon becomes more desirable than it might otherwise be.

'OK,' the voice agreed. 'May UG's feet turn purple and rot like cabbages! But *I* get to keep the spoon. I have been wanting a spoon for so many years... The dragon is very close to death.'

'What are you going to do?' whispered Hiccup.

'I'm going to open him up,' said the voice in the dark gleefully.

'But won't that *kill* him?' asked Hiccup, in a frenzy of anxiety. He had been hoping that she could just give Toothless some medicine to make him better.

'What's it to you?' jeered the voice. 'It's UG's dragon...'

'UG is very very fond of this dragon,' warned Hiccup, 'and he will be very very angry if something happens to him...'

'Oh, don't worry,' cackled the voice, and it was such a nasty noise, 'I'll sew him up again afterwards...'

Hiccup had heard of
such operations before, but he
had never seen one happen.

'But... but... how will you do it in
the dark?' stammered Hiccup.

'I can sew in the dark... I can weave
in the dark. I can write in the dark. When
you spend twenty years in the dark, your hands
become your eyes,' said the witch.

Rustling in the darkness again, a sound of
someone standing up, and rummaging through
things, and a scraping and a sharpening of
knives, and a tense concentration as a needle
was threaded.

'Will it hurt him?' asked Hiccup, in an
agony of anxiety.

'SOFT,' jeered the voice, 'You are
soft... Feel him... he's beyond pain...'

Poor Toothless was indeed now in
a deep coma, his little mouth ajar,
his spines soft and floppy and his
chest barely rising beneath
Hiccup's fingers.

'I've got some sleepyherb I can give him, if you like, weakling...' said the witch. Hiccup could hear her shuffling closer and sitting next to him. She had a most unpleasant smell.

'Hold him very still. Otherwise accidents could happen. This is a very sharp knife,' she said with relish. 'I like to keep my knives sharp, for gutting the rats.'

Poor Hiccup didn't really trust the witch... why would he? But what other choice did he have? And she really seemed to want the spoon.

So he held Toothless still while the witch held the sleepyherb under the little dragon's nose. The sleepyherb had a strong bitter smell that made Hiccup's eyes water, and Toothless stopped moving entirely.

That was an extraordinary moment. The entire operation took place in the absolute blackness of the prison cell.

Strong, skilful bony fingers working in the darkness, with a sharp knife, and a needle-and-thread, and herbs that smelled, and a witch's cool, unpleasant, but highly intelligent brain.

Hiccup sat as still as a statue, every

muscle tense with anxiety.

Five minutes was all it took,
and then she grunted, and handed Hiccup
something, saying, 'Wipe that on my cloak,'
and Hiccup could sense she was sewing up
Toothless's stomach again.

And in Hiccup's hand was the large, peculiar
shaped object that the witch had found inside
Toothless's belly.

Hiccup rubbed it hurriedly on the witch's cloak,
for it was a bit yucky.

No wonder Toothless hadn't been feeling very well.

For Hiccup was holding in his fingers Stoick's
magic stone, attached to which were a number of
other metal objects that Toothless had eaten over the
years. A spoon, a fork, a ring, a bolt, a key, several
coins and Valhallarama's earring and various other
little metal items that Toothless in his greed had
accidentally gobbled up under the mistaken
impression that they were FOOD.

All of these little metal items were stuck to
the magic stone at odd angles so that it
resembled a little metal star that had sat
hidden inside the darkness of his belly.

'I wonder why this dragon is so important to UG?' mused the voice to itself as it worked away on the stitching. 'It has an old scar on its chest in exactly the same place as…'
The voice trailed off. 'It's very strange… it's very strange… it's in exactly the same place… what a coincidence… it could be an accident… but there ARE no accidents…'

The witch finished the last stitch, and grunted with satisfaction. 'Haven't lost my touch,' she said. Grasping bony fingers reached into Hiccup's lap and pulled the spoon off the magic stone. 'MY spoon, I think,' she said greedily.

And then… 'He'll live.'

And there was the sound of her retreating to another part of the cell.

Hiccup could feel a little jerk of the body he was holding in his hands.

Toothless stirred and moved.

'You're alive!' breathed Hiccup, picking him up and resting him on his shoulder, 'You're alive!'

Hiccup could feel the beginnings of a puff of smoke drifting past his chin, and Toothless croaked very weakly and groggily, 'W-w-where are we?'

170

'We're in this tree...' Hiccup started to answer in Dragonese – and stopped.

There was a silence in the tree that just prickled with suspicion.

You could almost hear the witch thinking, *Who are you?*

So Hiccup said very hurriedly, 'Um, thank you for healing UG's dragon for me. I was thinking of trying to get out of here without waiting for UG's men... because... because... I have to get somewhere in a bit of a hurry... is up there the only way out?'

When the witch spoke, her voice was dry as dust.

'After twenty years of searching,' said the witch, 'my conclusion is that that IS the only way out. And it is locked. Get used to waiting boy, is my advice, get used to waiting.' And the voice settled back in the darkness.

Hiccup stroked Toothless automatically. It is very unnerving being in a small cell with a witch you cannot see.

'What are you thinking?' said Hiccup.

'I am thinking,' said the witch, 'that your name is not Fishlegs.'

Oh dear, thought Hiccup, *oh dear oh dear oh dear oh dear.*

It was very difficult to carry on a conversation with a witch when what he was REALLY wanting to do was run around shrieking: 'GET ME OUT OF HERE!'

For the witch could see in the dark.

And he could not.

But Hiccup knew that the witch was suspicious now, and the only thing to do was to keep her talking. Witches loved a battle of wits.

'Cor-rect,' said Hiccup, 'and *I* am thinking that your name is not Hogtrude.'

The witch laughed, a wheezy, croaky sound. 'Cor-rect,' said the witch. 'But who *am* I? I'll tell you what, Boy-Whose-Name-Is-Not-Fishlegs, you seem a sharp lad, and I have all the time in the world on my hands, so I will strike a bargain with you. Let us have a battle of wits. I will tell you a story, and at the end of the story, we will each have ONE guess at who the other person is. Whoever guesses right, gets to kill the other.'

'OK…' said Hiccup. 'And what if I don't want to do this battle of wits?'

'I kill you anyway,' said the witch. (Hiccup knew she was going to say that.)

'In which case I accept,' said Hiccup.

'I thought you would. The
story I am about to tell you,' said
the voice, bitter as bitter, 'is the reason
UG put me in here in the first place.'

'UG put you in here because you told
him a story?' asked Hiccup in surprise, trying to
listen and think of escape plans at the same time.

'That's right…' purred the witch. Now her voice
was like a drop of vinegar on the tongue.

And so in the absolute black darkness of
the tree in the heart of Berserk… with Toothless
slowly recovering on his shoulder… listening while
desperately trying to think how he was going to get out
of here… *this* was where Hiccup finally learned the
Secret of the Lost Throne of the Wilderwest.

Here is the story that the witch told him.

The story that made UG the Uglithug put her in
prison for twenty years.

And it had to be said, she was a horrible woman,
but she knew how to tell a story.

14. THE LOST THRONE OF THE WILDERWEST

'For many years, the Barbaric Archipelago was run by the Kings of the Wilderwest,' began the voice of the witch in the darkness. 'The King was the fiercest, the boldest, the most ferocious of the Chiefs of the Barbaric Archipelago, and for many years, the position was held by the Chief of the Hooligan Tribe.

'Grimbeard the Ghastly was the last of these Kings, the toughest and most ruthless pirate the Archipelago had ever seen, and his kingdom stretched as far as the eye could see. He even fought and defeated the King of the Mainland, and forced him into exile, so that Grimbeard the Ghastly's lands included not only these islands, but the vast Mainland territories inland.

'Grimbeard the Ghastly enslaved every human who wasn't a Viking, and he was such a successful pirate that he became disgustingly rich. The little island of Berk was no longer big enough for him. With the help of thousands of slaves, and dragons in chains, he built a great city on the island of Tomorrow.

'All was going well for Grimbeard. He had a son, Thugheart, the spitting image of himself. And another son, Chucklehead, who was the spitting image of Thugheart.

'He was a happy, violent man, who cheerfully robbed his neighbours, ate heartily, drank heartily, fought like a cornered bear, and loved nobody but himself.

'His third son was born, on the 29th of February, a Leap Year...

'He was a bonny baby who slipped out of his mother without a sound, bright blue eyes wide open with an expression of eager surprise in them, and a shock of bright blond hair. Even as a newborn, he seemed to be looking about him with a sense of joyous adventure, a sense of the excitement of everything about him.

'He did not realise that he was not destined to enjoy the world for very long. For he was too small, you see. He was a runt.'

Hiccup had forgotten already that he didn't want to hear this story. He interrupted indignantly at this point. 'What do you mean he was a *runt*?'

'I mean he was a RUNT,' said the voice hatefully. 'They took him to the Naming Dame and they were hoping she would call him Fatlegs or Dragonheart, or something Viking-y, but she could see

175

instantly what the poor besotted parents couldn't see and she named him HICCUP.'

'Why did she name him HICCUP?' asked Hiccup, trying to sound casual and just mildly interested. He already had a horrible feeling that the witch had guessed who he was, Thor only knows how. Or why was she telling him this story about his own Tribe, his own ancestors?

'Because that's what they call the RUNTS in the Hooligan Tribe,' said the witch impatiently. 'Hiccup means "accident", you see. Well, of course the moment the Naming Dame named him a runt, everybody knew he had to be got rid of. For if a RUNT survives till adulthood in the Hooligan Tribe, he brings with him an unlucky Fate, the Fate of changing the course of history.

'Hiccup Horrendous Haddock the First had caused his father to lose his entire kingdom in the rich farmlands of the east, so that the Hooligan Tribe had to settle in the barren island wastes of the Archipelago.

'*This* boy would have to be named Hiccup Horrendous Haddock the Second, and there was a good chance that he would bring the same bad luck on his family as the first Hiccup.'

Hiccup's heart beat fast in the darkness. Hiccup

had only recently found out that he had a Secret Ancestor, Hiccup Horrendous Haddock the Second, who had been a Dragonwhisperer like himself.* Now he was sitting here, hearing his story.

Goosebumps prickled all over Hiccup's head.

'Grimbeard was nothing if not a stern man,' continued the witch. 'He had no intention of letting his son live to bring bad luck on his family in the same way as the first Hiccup. It was a shame and whatnot, but he already had Thugheart and Chucklehead, after all. So he allowed the boy to be named HICCUP HORRENDOUS HADDOCK THE SECOND in a very elaborate naming ceremony, while secretly making plans for the baby's murder. He knew that his son needed to be exposed on the mountainside, in accordance with Hooligan tradition. He also knew that his wife Chinhilda, a spirited woman who was handy with an axe, would not necessarily agree with this course of action.

'Women could be so unreasonable.

'So with his own hands Grimbeard stole the sleeping baby from his sleeping wife's breast... He climbed on board his Riding-Dragon, and he flew to a neighbouring island, where he left his sleeping son, his own flesh and blood, on a mountainside to perish.

---

* Hiccup found this out in *A Hero's Guide to Deadly Dragons*.

He left him there under a little bush of heather that dripped down like tears on the baby's crib. And then he climbed back on his Riding-Dragon and soared off without so much as a backward glance, for Grimbeard had never particularly liked babies, and when it cried, as babies will, this one resembled nothing so much as a screaming tomato. A rather SMELLY screaming tomato. To tell the truth, he had felt sadder when he had to put down one of his favourite Rottdragons, who had been injured in a fight. As he flew back over the salty waves towards his beautiful city on the island of Tomorrow, he wondered what would be for supper tonight. Pig's trotters, he hoped. That was his favourite.

'Chinhilda did not accept Grimbeard's perfectly reasonable explanation. She was so angry when she awoke that she picked up her sword and attacked him then and there. Grimbeard the Ghastly won the swordfight, but refused to kill her. She then broke down in tears, and begged him to tell her where he had left the baby. Which was very annoying of her, because it made Grimbeard feel uncomfortable, and he hated to feel uncomfortable. He refused to tell her of course, and got his guards to drag her out of his presence so that he could enjoy his pig's trotters in peace and quiet. As they dragged her away, she cursed him – a terrible curse, for it was the curse of a sorceress – and left in her boat to look for her lost son. For many many years, her white boat could be seen, looking and looking for the lost baby. Until finally it was seen no more. It is said that her ghost still haunts the Bay of the Broken Heart…'

'Oh, for Thor's sake…' said Hiccup. 'I thought that was just a story…'

'Stories come from somewhere,' said the witch. 'The past haunts the present in more ways than we realise.

'Grimbeard was rather relieved to have been let off so lightly.

'He could now get on with his fighting, and his eating, and his drinking without her nagging him, or crying at him.

'But to his surprise, Grimbeard found that he wasn't enjoying the burglary, and the fighting, and the drinking, and the eating quite as much as he used to.

'Even the beer didn't taste the same.

'He couldn't understand it.

'He got rid of his cook, and hired a new one, but it didn't make any difference.

'The beer was less beery, and the pig's trotters less piggy, and none of those idiot Warriors could put up half as good a battle as Chinhilda in a swordfight.

'He ate a little more of the pig's trotters, and put on ten pounds, and that just gave him indigestion.

'What could be the matter with him?

'And that was the beginning of the Curse.

'The baby, Hiccup Horrendous Haddock the Second, was a hopeful little thing by nature, so for a while he lay there happily, admiring the beauty of the night sky, and waiting for someone to pick him up. And after a while he realised that nobody WAS coming to pick him up, so he let out an exploratory little cry. And then when nobody answered THAT, for some time the baby cried furiously, angrily, red with temper. It was lucky that there were no passing predators to hear him. He kicked off his covers with his cross little legs, and then he got cold, and cried harder still. Eventually he gave up all hope, and lay shaking with fear, his little nose running, his face wet with snot and tears. Now he knew he had been abandoned, he sensed he should be quiet. Every now and then he would moan softly to himself, and gnaw hungrily on his tiny knuckles.

'He shook his wobbly little legs up at the cold uncaring heavens, brilliant with stars.

'*We do not care about you…* said the stars. *You*

will have to look after yourself…

'And then the baby let out a whimper of fear.

'A great face loomed over him.

'A face that blotted out the night sky.

'The face of a gigantic male Grimler Dragon, with the cold yellow eyes of a Great White Shark and a smile so grim it might as well have been the most deadly of frowns.

'The male Grimler Dragon was unhappy, and it was hungry, and it opened its mouth, edged with fangs as sharp and as long as a Hooligan sword.

'But then it changed its mind.

'It took hold of the straps on the baby's crib, and flew off with it into the night sky. Up and up, to a cave in the mountaintop, where a female Grimler Dragon lay dying, her yellow eyes growing dimmer and dimmer in the darkness. She was licking the cold stiff body of her stillborn baby, even though she knew it would never wake again. All around the dead baby were the sad broken remains of its shell.

'The gigantic male entered the cave cautiously, his mighty head held down low, the crib swinging from his closed jaws.

'The female lashed out at him, dying candle eyes alight with fury, hissing like an infuriated cobra and missing his jugular by centimetres. Even a dying Grimler is mortally dangerous. "Get away from me, worm of no account!"

'The male dropped the crib in front of her and backed away to the entrance of the cave.

'The female lifted her arm to swipe away the crib... and then paused as she heard the crying from within. With a tremendous effort, she lifted her weak head and peered inside. "What is this you bring me?" she spat. "A HUMAN baby? A mud-bound, wing-less, green-blood-killing, HUMAN child??" Spluttering in outrage, she lifted her talons to kill it... and paused as it cried again.

'Her great clawed hand, shaking uncontrollably, reached into the crib and drew out the baby. He was warm. He was alive.

'The wriggling baby forgot to be scared and rubbed his little cheek against her smooth snakeskin chest, searching for food.

'She looked down at him, an unreadable expression in her eyes.

'He was limp with hunger. His face was streaked with tears. He was small and completely vulnerable.

'The female Grimler's forked tongue licked the baby's cheek.

'Gently, she drew the human baby down to her pouch, where her milk ducts were waiting.*

'The male Grimler Dragon sat watching her from the entrance of the cave, as still as if he had been turned to stone. Eventually, when the female's concentration was completely absorbed in fussing over the feeding baby, he crept forward and gently took the body of his dead child in his hand. The female dragon pretended not to notice. The light in her eyes was growing stronger.

'The male left her there, in the quiet darkness of the cave, and took off from the clifftops. He buried his child deep in the marshes.

'So that was how Hiccup Horrendous Haddock the Second grew up to speak Dragonese.'

All sorceresses make excellent storytellers, and Hiccup was now so caught up in the story of his Ancestor that he interrupted without even thinking. He had forgotten the battle of wits. He had forgotten everything...

'You mean... Hiccup Horrendous Haddock the Second learnt to speak Dragonese BECAUSE HE WAS BROUGHT UP BY DRAGONS?' stammered Hiccup Horrendous Haddock the Third in disbelief and excitement.

---

* Most dragons did not suckle their young. They fed them regurgitated food after hatching, like birds. But the Hiccup memoirs have spoken before of dragons that had developed marsupial and mammal-like characteristics. The Grimler Dragon must have been one of these.

'That's exactly what I mean,' said the witch.

'But… but… but…' Hiccup asked, 'how did he learn to speak Norse? How did he get back to his human family?'

The witch continued with the story.

'A Hooligan Raiding Party was on its way east. It set up camp on the island. They were hunting for food, and came across this little wild boy, now about seven years old, hissing like a serpent and flapping his arms at them as if they were wings. He was hunting with his younger dragon-brother, Furious, also adopted by the Grimler Dragons. Furious was a Seadragonus Giganticus Maximus, so even though he was still a baby, he was already the size of a small elephant. Despite the size difference, Furious worshipped the boy, as younger brothers will. They took the boy and the dragon to Grimbeard in a cage. And Grimbeard only had to take one LOOK at the child to realise who he was. The bright blond hair… the bright blue eyes… Grimbeard knew who he was, all right.

'And, of course, he couldn't kill the boy NOW. That would have been very bad luck indeed. For the child had survived being exposed on the mountainside, and that was a sign from the gods that he was destined for survival.

'So, whether he liked it or not, Grimbeard felt he had to bring the boy up as his son.'

'And what was he like, Hiccup Horrendous Haddock the Second?' asked Hiccup Horrendous Haddock the Third curiously.

'He was a pest,' said the witch, 'like the First Hiccup before him. Always asking difficult questions. Completely fearless, very cheeky, afraid of nothing and nobody. I have to admit, although he began as a runt, he grew up strong. He was a born leader, charismatic, strong, handsome, the best at everything, sword-fighting, wrestling, Insults, chess-playing, the lot.'

'Oh,' said Hiccup, very disappointed. He rather wanted Hiccup Horrendous Haddock the Second to be like HIM.

'They called him "the Dragon-whisperer" because of course he spoke Dragonese even more fluently than he spoke Norse. Grimbeard was a stern man... but after losing Chinhilda, he found he was weaker than he thought he was. Despite himself, he grew fond of the boy who looked so like his mother, but had Grimbeard's own courage and swagger. He was always very jealous of the boy's love for dragons, and banned him from speaking Dragonese. Hiccup Horrendous

Haddock the Second took no notice of THAT, of course. He was very wild, always fighting and rebelling against his father. He would break into the Library at every opportunity... he released all his father's slaves on at least three different occasions, and of course in the END...'

'What happened in the end?' asked Hiccup.

'*Tragedy*,' whispered the voice of the witch with triumph in the darkness. 'No good could ever come of a boy who loved dragons more than he did his human flesh and blood. Hiccup Horrendous Haddock the Second believed passionately that dragons should not be enslaved by humans. And so... the stupid boy organised a Great Dragon Petition, a Petition that would be peaceful and would be led by Hiccup's dragon-brother, Furious, whom he had grown up with in the cave, and who had now grown to be a mighty force indeed.

'He knew that he couldn't appeal to Grimbeard's softer side, because Grimbeard didn't have a softer side. Grimbeard was impressed by STRENGTH, and strength alone. So Hiccup's idea was that thousands upon thousands of dragons should gather together in a demonstration of strength and solidarity, and demand their freedom all together. The

demonstration would be
peaceful. Hiccup Horrendous
Haddock the Second did not intend
to harm his father in any way – he was too
soft for that,' said the witch scornfully. 'He
thought himself such a *Hero*...

'But Thugheart learnt of the Petition.
He was jealous of his father's love for Hiccup
Horrendous Haddock the Second. The final
straw was when Grimbeard gave Hiccup a lucky
amber amulet* of great price. Thugheart secretly
told his father that Hiccup was rebelling against
him, and was sending a dragon army to kill him.'

'What a liar!' said Hiccup indignantly.

'Yes, it was clever of Thugheart, wasn't it?'
grinned the witch. 'The dragons arrived when
Grimbeard the Ghastly was playing against his
son Hiccup Horrendous Haddock the Second
in a game of chess. Grimbeard the Ghastly
had ordered his troops to fire on the
dragons as soon as they saw them... and
thus it was that a peaceful Petition
turned into a bloody battle.

'Beside himself with anger that
his son had betrayed him,

---

* An 'amulet' was a lucky charm.

Grimbeard the Ghastly took out
his sword, the Stormblade… and ran
Hiccup Horrendous Haddock the Second
through on the spot.'

'NO!' Hiccup Horrendous Haddock the
Third gasped, and put his hands over his ears.

'Yes,' said the witch with grim satisfaction.

'As Hiccup Horrendous Haddock the Second
lay dying, he looked his father straight in the eyes.
"A dying man does not lie, father," said Hiccup
Horrendous Haddock the Second. "Thor knows, we
have not always seen eye to eye, but I swear on my
Hero's honour that I meant no harm to you or to your
crown. The dragons came in peace rather than war…"

'The mighty Dragon Furious swooped down,
intending to kill Grimbeard in revenge, but Hiccup
stopped him. "Do not kill him, Furious!" he said.
"Promise me you will not kill him! I will not have my
father's blood on my hands!"

'Furious held back his fire, and Grimbeard the
Ghastly looked into his son's eyes and knew it was
the truth. He dropped the Stormblade in terror,
and desperately tried to stem the red blood pouring
out of his son's chest with his own, brown,
soldier's hands.

188

'But his hands were too
small to cover up the wound that
they had made.

'Time ticked on, and could not
run backwards, even for so great a King as
Grimbeard the Ghastly.

'It was the second time Grimbeard the
Ghastly had tried to kill his son.

'And this time he succeeded.

'Hiccup Horrendous Haddock the Second died
in his father's arms.

'Grimbeard the Ghastly held the un-breathing
body up to the heavens, and howled in horror...

'*Too late... too late...*

'Furious swooped down, wrenched the body of
his brother from Grimbeard's arms, and flew east with
it clasped in his talons.

'The peaceful Dragon Petition had turned into
a terrible battleground.

'Grimbeard the Ghastly's troops were under
fire not only from the dragons, but also from
Thugheart's own men, who were using the chaos
to try and seize the throne. Thugheart's forces
were joined by those of the Uglithug King
of the Mainland.

'Even in despair,
Grimbeard was a mighty soldier.
The dragons were weakened by the
distress of their Leader, Furious. By evening,
Grimbeard had won, over dragons and
Thugheart and the King of the Mainland – but at
what terrible cost. The city was in flaming ruins,
and thousands of men and dragons lay dead.

'Grimbeard was distraught with grief, and so
furious that he laid a Curse on the Throne of the
King of the Wilderwest, and threw it into the Ocean.
He set fire with his own hands to the last remains of
his city. He buried the crown and the Stormblade. He
cursed his treasure, and hid it in the deepest cavern
he could possibly find.*

'Grimbeard sent the remains of his Tribe
back to the little Isle of Berk, with his second son,
Chucklehead to rule over a much diminished
kingdom.

'His last act as King was to banish his
treacherous son Thugheart to the Outcast Lands.

'And then he set sail into the west in
his ship *The Endless Journey*, and

---

* Please read *How to Be a Pirate* to see
if Hiccup finds Grimbeard's treasure.

was never seen again.

'And that was the last of the Kings of the Wilderwest. The Archipelago was broken up into a hundred warring Tribes again. The Uglithugs snatched the huge section of the Kingdom that spread miles and miles to the east. And so it has remained ever since.'

Silent tears were running down Hiccup Horrendous Haddock the Third's face. 'That's awful...' said Hiccup. 'So Hiccup Horrendous Haddock the Second actually died... he didn't wake up at the last minute? That is such a sad story...'

'It isn't *a* story,' snapped the witch. 'It's *history*. Of course it's tragic. This is real life, not a fairy tale... but *that* isn't the Secret bit...'

The witch began to whisper, although nobody could possibly hear them in the heart of that tree trunk in the middle of the jungle.

'The Secret is a Prophecy. A Prophecy about the new King... the new King of the Wilderwest... a King who shall bring together the Tribes of the Archipelago, who shall make us great again... who shall rule over ALL with glory and with POWER!'

The witch laughed. 'Only *I*
know this Prophecy. And of course
UG doesn't want there to be a King of
the Wilderwest. Why would he? A new
King of the Wilderwest might take back the
land the Uglithugs burgled long, long ago…'
Hiccup swallowed hard.

'The Prophecy was written by Grimbeard
the Ghastly himself as he departed on his final
journey. The first verse goes like this:

'Only the King can sit on the Throne
Only my Heir can lift the Curse
In his hand my Second-Best Sword
Around his neck the lucky amulet…'

The witch stopped. 'Only I know the rest.'
Hiccup was feeling very, very sick.
'I'll tell you who the New King is
going to be, if you like,' whispered the
witch.

Hiccup swallowed even harder.
'Alvin the Treacherous,'
whispered the witch in
the darkness.

'NO!' said Hiccup. 'NO! NO! NO!'

'Yes,' said the witch. 'For Alvin is the direct descendant of Thugheart, the first of the line of Treacherous. I believe the Prophecy refers to *him*.'

Casually, Hiccup asked, 'And what about Grimbeard's *other* Heirs? The descendants of Grimbeard's son Chucklehead? Could the Prophecy be referring to any of THEM?'

The witch made a revolting spitting noise. 'Oh, it can't possibly be about *them*... the Prophecy talks about somebody *clever* and they're idiots the lot of them... strong but stupid. According to Destiny the latest of them, an ignoramus called Stoick the Vast, has married Grimhilda the Gormless and they have had three reassuringly stupid children.'

'So according to Destiny Stoick wasn't supposed to marry *Valhallarama*?' squeaked Hiccup.

'Valhallarama of the White Arms?'

said the voice of the witch in excitement. 'No, Valhallarama has been destined since birth to marry Humungously Hotshot the Hero...' Her voice crackled through the room with the keenness of a whip. 'So... I was right... something happened to interrupt Destiny... some sort of MEDDLING occurred?' she asked Hiccup. 'Some sort of ACCIDENT? What was it? What was it? What was it?'

The words hissed out like a whole nest of serpents.

'No, no,' said Hiccup quickly. 'Now I come to think of it, Stoick the Vast is *of course* married to Grimhilda the Gormless...'*

---

* But of course, Hiccup knew that Valhallarama had never married Humungously Hotshot the Hero. She had married Hiccup's father, Stoick the Vast, instead And it was Alvin HIMSELF who had interrupted Destiny. If you want to find out how, you will have to read the fifth episode of Hiccup's memoirs, *How to Twist a Dragon's Tale*.

But it was too late.

The story had done its work.

Carried away by its power, Hiccup had betrayed himself and his identity.

'I'm going to guess!' shrieked the witch gleefully. 'I'm going to guess! You,' hissed the voice of the witch with biting spite and triumph, 'you, are the Third Hiccup... you are the Boy-Who-Never-Should-Have-Been... you are the one whom Destiny has sent me to devour in the darkness... *you* are HICCUP...

HORRENDOUS... HADDOCK... THE THIRD.'

'Yes,' said Hiccup, starting to shake. 'Yes, but—'

'I WIN! I WIN!' shouted the witch, in an ecstasy of excitement.

'*Wait!*' said Hiccup urgently, '*I have a guess too!*'

'And what,' said the witch sarcastically, 'is *your* guess, then?'

'*You,*' said Hiccup Horrendous Haddock the Third, as a thousand names jostled through his mind in a second.

'*You,*' – said Hiccup as the witch sighed, 'I'm wa-a-a-aiting.' – '*You,*' said Hiccup Horrendous Haddock the Third as *one* name popped into his mind, who knows from where, in a glorious moment of clarity, '*You*… are Alvin's mother.'

The witch gave a shriek of fury.

'IS THAT CORRECT?' shouted Hiccup to the blackness around him. '*IS THAT CORRECT?*'

'It is…' hissed the witch, a soft, dying sound.

'WHAT DO WE DO
NOW, THEN?' shouted Hiccup.

Silence.

'HELLO?' said Hiccup, taking a
good grip on his sword and trying to peer
into the terrible darkness all around him.
'WHAT DO WE DO NOW? HELLO???'

Silence. A dread coldness came over Hiccup.
He knew what they had to do now.

Absolute blackness all around him. So black,
it was as if he were blind.

Each had the right to kill the other.

And the witch could see in the dark.

'I'm o-o-over he-e-e-re....' came the sing-
song voice of the witch.

Hiccup spun round.

Oh for Thor's sake. For Thor's sake.

Hiccup lunged.

The sound of the witch laughing.

'Be-h-I-I-I-I-ind you....' sang the
witch, from a completely different
part of the tree-trunk cell, and
Hiccup whirled round, and
lunged with his sword,

and met nothing
but black air.

Hiccup stood there, panting
and sweating in the blackness. He
knew she was there somewhere.

But where?

Silence.

Hiccup whirled again, and lunged.

Nothing.

She was close, she was close, he
could *sense* she was close…

He could smell her, he was sure
he could, he could feel her near –
and sobbing, he lashed out and
wildly plunged this way and that,
losing control as his sword met
the airy darkness of nothing at
all. Terror crept like black
beetles over

his scalp and… with a
slight, snuffly, smoky wheeze,
Toothless FINALLY woke up.

Toothless's eyes had been
closed the whole time they had been
in the tree.

And now, as his eyelids snapped
open, the frail light of his eyebeams
shone out in the darkness…

… illuminating the ghastly
grinning figure of the upstanding
witch, standing RIGHT OVER
Hiccup, close enough to touch,
with her sword raised ready to
bring down and strike.

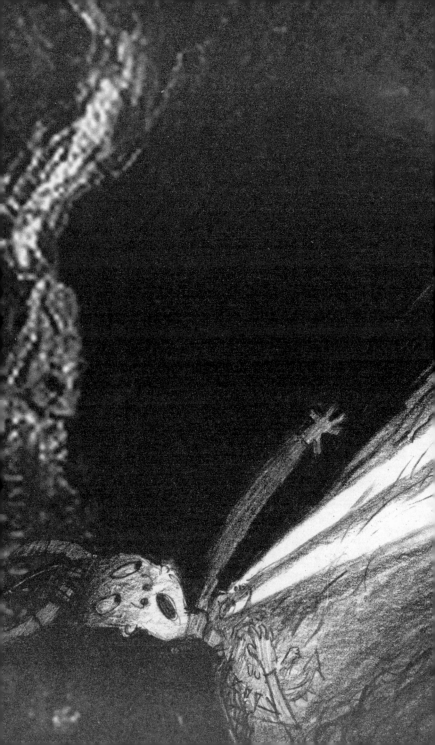

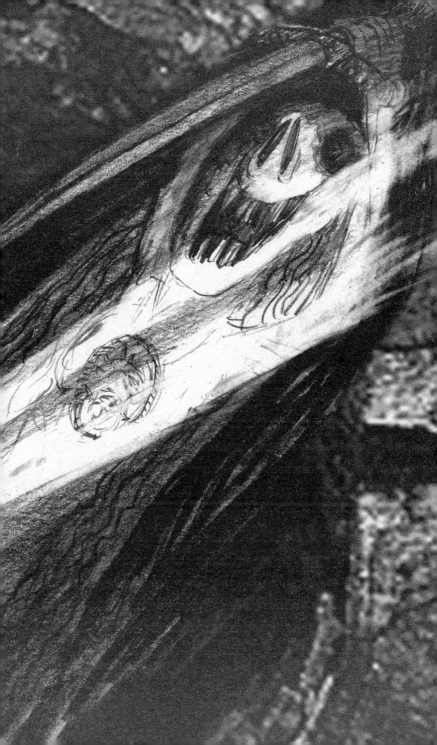

One second later and Hiccup would have been dead.

But the witch had not seen daylight in twenty years.

And the light of Toothless's eyebeams blinded her like poison.

She let out an awful scream, dropping her sword and putting her hands over her eyes with a wail of pain, rubbing at them, tearing at them, to shut out the light.

Frantic with terror, Hiccup looked around the tree cell for some way, ANY way to get out of there.

The first light in twenty years fell faintly from Toothless's half-opened eyebeams on to jumbled heaps of rags, bottles, knives and spinning wheels, chewed up bones and speaking runes.

And, lying on the floor, just touching Hiccup's foot, was the funny collection of metal objects that had been inside Toothless's tummy, only a little before.

One of the objects was a KEY.

15. A BIG THANK YOU TO THE HYSTERIC TRIBE

Quick as winking, as the witch wailed and clutched her eyes, Hiccup reached to the floor and picked the key up. 'Keep your eyes *open*, Toothless!' yelled Hiccup, and he ran to the ladder.

Of course, it could have been any old key.

The key to Stoick's weapons cupboard, or the Dragon Stables, or the big chest under Stoick's bed where he kept his sword and other valuables.

But in that flash of light, Hiccup remembered where Toothless had been when he swallowed this particular key.

It had been in the Great Hall of Norbert the Nutjob.*

The Nutjobs of Hysteria were the dreamers and inventors of the Archipelago.

If I were going to build myself a great prison on Berserk, thought Hiccup, *who would I get to build it for me?*

---

* Please read *How to Cheat a Dragon's Curse*.

A Hysteric, that's who.

So Hiccup grabbed the key, and scrambled up the shredded rags of the shaking, quaking rope ladder, Toothless clinging to his shoulders, still half asleep and whimpering. And wailing like a siren, the blind witch followed.

Babbling with fear, Hiccup reached the top of the ladder, and with trembling fingers tore the key from the magic stone.

The witch was hard behind him now, screaming a high weird scream.

Hiccup fitted the key inside the lock of the barred door.

Bony fingers closed around his ankle.

The key turned, the door opened.

And the full moon shone on the witch's face.

She screeched again, crumpling before that light like a folding piece of paper, and with one kick of his ankle, Hiccup shook her off and back down into the darkness, and himself up and into the moonlight, and heaved the door shut BANG! CRASH! and SHUT... HER... IN.

Hiccup threw his body against the door as if to make absolutely sure it was totally shut. He stood there, panting, spread-eagled like a starfish, and gasping for air, great precious lungfuls of sweet moonlit air.

Oh thank Thor. Oh thank Thor.

Hiccup listened, and no sound was coming from below.

Pure silence.

The witch must be dead.

Alvin's Mother...

He couldn't really comprehend what had just happened.

It explained everything.

He remembered once when his grandfather, old Wrinkly, had told him that the greater the Hero, the more obstacles they had before them. Old Wrinkly called it 'becoming a Hero the Hard Way'.

And Hiccup hadn't believed him.

But now he knew who he was.

And he knew there was a chance that this Prophecy about the King of the Wilderwest might be referring to him, small, skinny Hiccup, the runt of the Hooligan Tribe.

But now it was all too much.

He wanted to forget the whole thing.

And with the witch dead, nobody but he knew about the Prophecy. And he certainly wasn't going to tell anyone.

For a moment Hiccup let himself enjoy the glorious triumph of defeating the witch.

Before remembering that Camicazi was still locked up somewhere in this forest.

How was he going to find her?

And then, the terrible, thumping, tattoo of his heart reminded him that Fishlegs and Humongous were about to be fed to the Beast in baskets in some horrible Ceremony of Human Sacrifice…

Toothless crawled up on to his chest and gave a great yawn, showing his little forked tongue. He had finally woken up, and he didn't have any idea of the drama that had just happened.

'Ooooh,' said Toothless happily. 'That nap made Toothless feel much *much* better.' He gave a satisfied little stretch. 'Toothless even HUNGRY. So. What are w-w-we doing now? Are we r-r-roosting?'

Scarers were beginning to gather around them in thick drifts of butterfly grey, attracted by the fear given off by Hiccup in the fight with the witch. 'We know you're afraaaaid…' they were singing in their little whispery voices. 'You c-a-an't fool u-u-u-us…'

Toothless put his face right up close so his eyes were eyeball-to-eyeball with Hiccup's and his two feet were placed tenderly on either side of Hiccup's face, as the boy stood spread-eagled in front of the door.

'Where *are* we?' asked Toothless with interest. 'Toothless thinks this may not be a g-g-good place to roost. It's a *bit* spooky,' said Toothless confidingly. 'H-h-have you noticed?'

Hiccup began to laugh, kind of hysterically. 'Yes, Toothless,' said Hiccup. 'I had noticed it was a bit spooky.'

'Sh-sh-shall we go home?' suggested Toothless.

'Yes, let's go home,' said Hiccup. 'But first we have to rescue the others.'

Hiccup shoved himself hard against the barred door as if he could trap all that he had learnt in the tree back down there in the darkness with the witch, and NEVER let it out.

And then he sheathed his sword, and began to run down the shaking rope bridges, with Toothless following him, squeaking, 'Others? W-w-what others? And why do we care? *We're* all right...' (dragons can be selfish) before letting out a shrill shriek as he caught sight of his own tummy, 'Aieee! We're *not* all right! Toothless w-w-wounded!' he squealed.

'You're fine, Toothless, you're fine... *now*,' said Hiccup, 'that was just where the witch in the tree opened you up...'

'A WITCH IN A TREE OPENED T-T-TOOTHLESS UP?' cried Toothless in round-eyed horror. 'Why d-d-didn't you stop her? You're s-s-supposed to look after Toothless!'

'Because... because... Toothless, it's a really long story, I'll explain later...

How do you find someone trapped in a tree that looks exactly the same as 35,672 other trees in the forest?

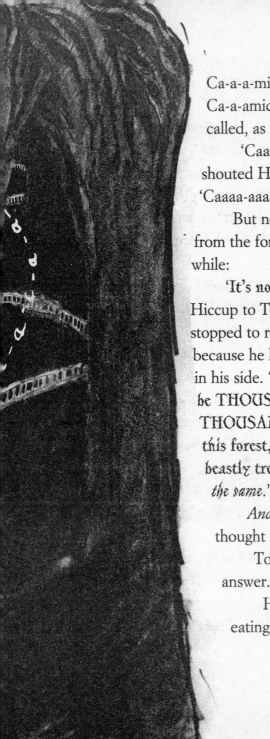

Ca-a-a-mica-a-a-azi!
Ca-a-amica-a-azi!!' Hiccup
called, as loud as he dared.
'Caaaaa-aaamicazi?'
shouted Hiccup again.
'Caaaa-aaaamicazi???'

But no answer came
from the forest. And after a
while:

'It's no good,' said
Hiccup to Toothless as he
stopped to rest for a moment,
because he had a stitch
in his side. 'There must
be THOUSANDS AND
THOUSANDS of trees in
this forest, and all these
beastly trees look *exactly*
the same.'

And we're lost,
thought Hiccup.

Toothless didn't
answer.

He was too busy
eating something,

perched on one of the struts of the rope bridge.

'I mean, how are we POSSIBLY going to find her?' said Hiccup, in panting despair. 'It's like looking for a particular type of *plankton* on a beach. I just have this horrible feeling that maybe this is FINALLY the time, FINALLY the adventure, where I run out of luck – *Toothless! What are you eating?*' scolded Hiccup. 'I can't believe you haven't learnt your lesson! IS THAT *EDIBLE?*'

'Is *f-f-fine*!' wailed Toothless. 'Horrible Mean Master get cross with poor Toothless. Look! Is not m-m-metal! It's a w-w-winkle!'

He held out the object that he had been gnawing at.

It was indeed a winkle, a favourite treat of all the hunting-dragons. They would stick their claws into the shells and draw out the little worms inside, and gobble them up alive, like squirming sweeties.

Yucky, but true.

Hiccup took the little brown shell off Toothless's claw.

'A winkle?' said Hiccup thoughtfully. Winkles lived in the sea, not two hundred and fifty feet up in the tree canopy.

'What is a winkle doing up *here?*' said Hiccup.

'There's l-l-l-loads of them...' said Toothless, pointing a helpful wing at the rotting mossy planks of the rope bridge.

And so there were.

Hiccup would not have noticed, so busy was he looking up at the treetops and shouting Camicazi's name. But now that Toothless's sharp little dragon eyes had pointed them out, there they were.

An intermittent trail of little tiny winkles, their warm brown shells glinting in the moonlight.

Sprinkled along the bridge at occasional intervals, as if they were a path that led somewhere...

And as Hiccup gazed at them, he thought of the fairy tale, of the boy being led into the forest to the house of a witch, and leaving a trail of little white stones so that he could find his way back.

Camicazi always kept a bag of winkles in her pocket as treats for her dragon, Stormfly.

What if Camicazi had dropped the winkles secretly as she was marched to her prison cell, so that a rescuer could follow her?

Camicazi was a rescourceful person, who thought on her feet like Hiccup. It would be just the type of thing that she might think of...

So with rising excitement, Hiccup followed the

trail of winkles, twisting and turning through the maze of rope bridges. Sometimes the path ran out for a while – but there was always another winkle, even if it was a way further on.

And of course, Toothless thought the whole thing was a lovely game. 'Don't eat them!' warned Hiccup sternly. 'We're going to need them to show us the way back to the Berserk Village.'

Until at last the winkles came to a dead stop, at a tree a lot smaller than the tree where Hiccup and Alvin's Mother had been imprisoned.

His heart in his mouth, Hiccup searched the ivy with feverish fingers.

And there it was, a door, cut into the tree.

Hiccup took out his key, and prayed to Thor that it would work.

He turned it… and as Hiccup had hoped, it was, indeed one of the Hysteric Tribe's miraculous inventions, *a key that opened all locks…*

Mentally, Hiccup sent a big thank you to the Hysteric Tribe. Mad as mackerel the lot of them, and highly dangerous, but they really were magnificent inventors.* There was a loud CLICK! And the door swung open with a cr-e-a-ak.

---

* Read *How to Ride a Dragon's Storm* to find out more of their inventions.

There was a trap-door inside, which Hiccup pulled up. He leant down into the tree as if he were calling down a well. 'CAMICAZI? CAMICAZI? CAMICAZI?'

A short silence.

Maybe she wasn't there, maybe he'd got it wrong, maybe he was too late –

And then a WHOOP of joy came echoing back up the tree trunk.

A whoop that cocky could only come from one person...

And sure enough, one minute later, Camicazi's unbelievably tangled hair and ferocious little face came poking up through the trap-door.

'Hiccup Horrendous Haddock the Third,' grinned Camicazi, with unmistakable relief.

Camacazill

I have to admit I'm really quite glad to see you...

'Camicazi,' grinned Hiccup.

'I have to admit,' said Camicazi, making a pretence of carelessness as she hopped out of the tree and dusted herself down. 'I'm really QUITE glad to see you.'

(From Camicazi, this was the equivalent of a huge tearful desperate hug.) 'I've escaped from practically every island in the Archipelago, but in THAT prison I couldn't pick the locks, none of my keys worked, there was nowhere to dig to and it was so DARK it was beginning to get me down... It wasn't that I was *frightened*,' she said aggressively.

'No, no, of course not,' said Hiccup quickly.

'But it was quite...' Her voice trailed off and she gave a little shiver.

Luckily Camicazi was the kind of character who didn't stay down for long. She was like an india-rubber ball that always pinged back into shape. Within two seconds of getting out her usual swagger returned.

'I mean, I daresay I'd have figured it out in the

216

end but… all the same, that was pretty impressive… for a *boy* and a Hooligan of course… what I want to say is… *thank you*,' said Camicazi.

'No problem,' said Hiccup. 'No problem at all.'

'And now,' said Camicazi, drawing her sword, 'I'm going to go after UG. HE was the one who captured me and brought me here. And he took my Stormfly back with him to his Uglithug Castle.'

You can't keep a BOG-BURGLAR UNDER LOCK AND KEY!

"I know a song that will get on your nerves, get on your nerves... g-g-get on your nerves... I know a song that will get on your nerves and this is how it g-g-goes..." (pause)... "I know a song that will g-g-get on your nerves..." and so

'Yes UG seems to be using the Berserks to get rid of his enemies for him,' said Hiccup. 'But first I'm afraid we have to get back to the Berserk Village fairly pronto. Fishlegs is in a bit of a tight spot...'

'Oh goodee,' said Camicazi. 'I don't mind taking a bit of a detour because I'm in the mood to spill some Berserk blood, I can tell you... those chain-bound, cheese-brained, wired-to-the-moon KIDNAPPERS! They'll regret the day they tried to put a padlock on the slippery heels and the airy fingers of a

Toothless was back to his old self ag

BOG-BURGLAR, I can tell you.'

'Well, ye-e-es,' said Hiccup, starting to run back in the direction of the Berserk Village. 'I can understand you might be feeling a bit cross with them, but don't forget there's only two of us, and there's… oh… maybe… a couple of thousand of *them*? We're a tad outnumbered… So I was thinking of just quietly releasing Fishlegs and these other people and then slipping away…'

'Two thousand EX-Berserks!' yelled Camicazi, frowning furiously. 'I'm going to kill them ALL! Starting with the fattest and working my way down!'

'Calm down, Camicazi,' suggested Hiccup. 'Everything's turning out pretty well suddenly. Half an hour ago it was all looking totally DESPERATE, but now… Toothless is cured, and *I* got away from the witch, and now I've found *you*, and I'm feeling hopeful that my luck has turned on this Quest, so keep your sword sheathed, and let's just Burgle them away, shall we, I think we've still got time…'

'Can't I at least kill a very very small one?' asked Camicazi, hugely disappointed. 'Oh go on, be a sport. It was so DARK in there and they really are total meanies.'

And so the two friends followed the trail of shining winkles across the maze of rope bridges, back towards the sleeping village of Berserk, with rising hope (in Hiccup at least) that this Quest might end happily for all, and with no bloodshed.

Hiccup might have thought differently if he could have seen the door back at the witch's tree he had left twenty minutes before.

He *should* have locked the door after him.

How could he have forgotten to do that?

For now there was a scratching from underneath that trap-door.

That could be mice, or rats, or a witch's bony fingernails.

And slowly, slowly, the door opened.

And two eyes peered out, scrunched up and streaming in pain from the moonlight.

The witch was ALIVE.

Hooligan Family Tree

GRIMBEARD THE GHASTLY
*O Hear His Name and Tremble,
Ugh, Ugh, Chief of the Hooligan
Tribe and King of the Wilderwest*

CHINHILDA
*Queen of the Wilderwest
and Ghost of the Bay
of the Broken Heart*

THUGHEART
*the founder and chief
of the Treacherous Tribe*

SYCHOFANTA
*of the sharp knife and the
Slippery Ways*

CHUCKLEHEAD

BUFFINTRUDA
the Flower of Bashem

HICCUP HORREENDOUS
HADDOCK II
the Dragon-whisperer

16. THE DEAD-OF-NIGHT CEREMONY

Hiccup and Camicazi followed the trail of winkles back through the maze of rope bridges, running as fast as they dared, with Toothless following at a slightly more leisurely pace as he ate up the winkles they left behind.

There was a slightly unnerving moment when Hiccup's foot went through the rotten wood of a plank on the bridge. But all was well. And as they drew nearer and nearer to the Berserk Village, Hiccup's hopeful mood changed. They were very very close to the start of the Ceremony.

The Full Moon was shining bright and expectant, the tree-dragons were chattering again, and even the bees, which had grown sleepy and quiet over the last couple of hours, were humming with a new urgency and excitement, as if something was about to happen.

'Quick, quick!' shouted Hiccup to Camicazi. 'We can still just make it…'

Surely they would get there in time? Now that everything was so very nearly all right…

But when Hiccup and Camicazi, gasping and panting, tattered and torn, finally reached the rope bridge that would carry them across to the tree village of Berserk, the Scarers erupted in a cacophony of noise.

'Awake! Awake! It's Dead-of-Night! It's Dead-of-Night!'

Just five minutes earlier, Hiccup could have unlocked every single one of those cages, and they could have slipped away into the darkness.

But now there was no time.

Hiccup threw himself across the last of the rope bridges and skidded across the mossy tree platform to the cages, where Humungously Hotshot and the Fiancés and Fishlegs were already awake.

1st Fiancé: 'Look! It's the latest Fiancé! He appears to be coming back!'

3rd Fiancé: 'You're going the wrong way, boy! Those nutters are waking up. Make off while you still can!'

1st Fiancé: 'YOU BETCHA!'

3rd Fiancé: 'TOO RIGHT...'

9th Fiancé: 'YESSIREE!'

'What are you doing, Hiccup? Turn back!' shouted out Humungously Hotshot.

'Unless, of course, you have a Plan...' urged Fishlegs from somewhere inside a cage so beset with

Scarers that it seemed like the cage was alive and covered with pale grey fur. 'A REALLY REALLY REALLY clever plan...'

Hiccup could see the torches were already being lit inside the tree-houses. Cries of 'UP THERE, HO!' and clanking of chains, and a leg and arm emerging from a door.

No time to free any of them.

'Camicazi! Go back home now!' shouted Hiccup.

'And miss all the fun? Who do you think you're giving orders to?' retorted Camicazi hotly. 'Go home yourself!'

'OK, climb a tree or something,' said Hiccup.

'Watchadoing? W-w-watchadoing?' squeaked Toothless in alarm. 'You're going the wrong w-w-way!' as Camicazi shimmied up the nearest tree with the agility of a cat and Hiccup jumped back IN to his own cage, and desperately re-locked the lock with the special key.

And as Hiccup flung the animal skins over his head, and began to do himself up in the chains again, Toothless flapped around his head in a frenzy of alarm and anxiety. 'You're s'posed to be e-e-escaping! This not escaping! Escaping is when you get OUT of things! Not INTO things!'

It was only in the nick of time, for the Berserks were up and yawning, and a particularly large, fat one so covered in chains he could barely walk gave a toot on a curly-wurly bugle three foot long and shouted out:

'LET THE DEAD-OF-NIGHT CEREMONY... BEGIN!!'

The Berserk treetop village was built around a clearing in the forest. An entire circle of bridges surrounded the clearing, forming a sort of tree amphitheatre, so that everybody could get a good view of the Ceremony.

Clattering and chattering, the Berserks made their way to their places on the rope bridges in their hundreds.

'PREPARE THE FIANCÉS!' yelled the Chief Berserk, and step, TAP, step, TAP, step TAP, clank clank – Alvin the Treacherous approached the cages.

At this point, Hiccup had the great satisfaction of sitting bolt upright, swaddled in his chains like a little metal mummy.

'AAAAAAAAARGH!' screeched Alvin the Treacherous, leaping backwards as if someone had bit him. His eye popped. 'WHAT... how did you... when did you... you're supposed to be... *what are* YOU doing here?'

Hiccup yawned. 'Well, I'm hanging
around waiting to be killed in some
spooky Dead-of-Night Ceremony of yours, of course,'
he replied. 'What did you expect me to be doing?
Playing chess? Looking for birds' eggs? Practising my
breaststroke? There's not a lot I CAN be doing, is
there, when I'm chained up inside this cage.'

'But... but... but... but...' stammered Alvin
the Treacherous, staring at Hiccup as if he had seen a
ghost.

'HURRY UP, ALPHONSE! BRING ON THE
FIRST VICTIM!' yelled the Chief Berserk.

The drumming began, the same drumming that
Hiccup had heard from a distance on the Beach of the
Broken Heart. It seemed a lifetime ago.

The entire Berserk Tribe had turned out to
watch the Ceremony. They lined the bridges of the
walkways, shaking their chains in excitement, howling
up at the sky and generally making a tremendous
racket. They were already beginning to lose themselves
in a Berserker rage, and one or two of them lost it
entirely in their excitement, and leapt over the edge of
the bridge into the depths below.

They began to stamp in unison on the rope
bridges, chanting:

DEAD-OF-NIGHT! DEAD-OF NIGHT! DEAD-OF NIGHT!

in time to the drumming.

And then louder, 'Dead-of-*Night*! Dead-of-*Night*! Dead-of-*Night*!'

And then louder still, 'DEAD-OF-NIGHT! FEED THE BEAST! DEAD-OF-NIGHT! FEED THE BEAST!'

FEED THE BEAST!

they

screamed.

It wasn't the noise of

the Berserkers that was so frightening, though.

It was the low grumble of noise that was coming

out of that leafy greenery down in the clearing, the insatiable gruntings and snorting of a hungry Beast, hidden below, knowing that it was feeding time. Hiccup's heart began to do cartwheels in his chest as he realised, too late, that he did not want to be fed to the Beast.

The Chief Berserk had removed some of his chains in honour of the occasion. He held up his hands for silence.

'O Mighty Thor,' yelled the old lunatic, 'hear the voices of us earthly nutters. It is Feeding Time for the Beast in the Heart of the Jungle. Accept this poor sacrifice, and make us as strong and as crazy in battle as you are yourself! Cheers!'

And the Berserk toasted the Full Moon in mead made from the bees of Berserk.

The Fiancés were determined to outdo each other in bravery, now that they knew that the end was nigh. They couldn't put their hands up but they LAUNCHED themselves at the bars of their cages in their excitement to be the first to go.

3rd Fiancé: 'ME FIRST! OH ME FIRST!'

1st Fiancé: 'Get back in line there, *I* was the first to be caught!'

10th Fiancé: 'Which means you made the worst

job of it, and therefore I should be the first to go, my heart really is broken, and I die a happy man for the love of Princess Tantrum!'

1st Fiancé: 'Oh put a sock in it, show-off…'

And so on.

'SHUDDUP!' screamed Alvin, forgetting his French accent in his fury.

What Alvin liked was BLUBBERING victims, not thirteen outrageously noble Fiancés arguing about who would get to be first to die.

'The boy is first,' sneered Alvin, 'because THIS TIME I have to make sure the little rat is truly dead.'

Hiccup was dragged out towards another cage. This one was attached to a long rope that was wound around a winch at the other end. He was tied, upside down and firmly, inside the cage, and the cage door was shut (the Berserks weren't taking any chances).

Alvin locked the cage door himself.

'Goodbye, Hiccup Horrendous Haddock the Third,' whispered Alvin the Treacherous, waving his good hand at the upside-down Hiccup.

'I *would* say, I'll meet you in Valhalla,' replied Hiccup through gritted teeth. 'But I don't think you'll be going there.'

Alvin laughed and slapped the side of the cage.

'Going down!'

To the cheers of the watching Berserks the cage was winched up, and then swung slowly out over the dense circle of green undergrowth, on a sort of wooden-arm-and-pulley system.

Then the Berserks began to rock back and forth rhythmically and hum to themselves, as slowly, slowly, slowly the cage was lowered into the jungle below.

'Oh for Thor's sake…' gasped Camicazi, clinging like a little black cat to her tree branch above. 'How on earth is he going to get out of THIS one?'

'What's happening?' shouted Fishlegs, because of course *he* couldn't see what was going on, through layers of Scarers six-deep.

'Hurrah!' shouted Humungously Hotshot the Hero.

'Has he escaped?' said Fishlegs eagerly, hope rising.

'No, no,' said Humungous. 'But he's being so BRAVE! What a Hero! It's an honour to have known him!'

Down, down, down went the cage. They could see the little upside-down figure of Hiccup, swinging within, like a poor bound bird tied to its perch. Toothless fluttered around, in a distracted sort of way. Scarers besieged the cage from all directions.

Goodbye, Hic**c**up
Horrendous Haddock
the Third...

Down,
down, down...
The cage hovered for a moment

over the wavy leafy green sea, like a
tantalising little worm being dangled
over the nose of a salmon or a pike
lurking below the surface.

It jiggled and danced enticingly.

'FEED THE BEAST! FEED THE
BEAST! FEED THE BEAST! FEED THE
BEAST! FEED THE BEAST! FEED THE
BEAST! FEED THE BEAST!' yelled the
Berserks in chanting, drumming, howling
unison, craning forward to look at the waving
sea of vegetation below.

Camicazi watched from her perch on
the tree branch.

'GO HICCUP GO!' she shouted
excitedly. Such was her trust in Hiccup
she really believed he could escape from
anything.

And other eyes were watching too.

*Witch's eyes, hiding in the shadows,
watchful, gaining in strength as they grew
accustomed to the moonlight…*

Meanwhile, inside the cage, as soon
as it began to lower into the jungle, Hiccup
was fiddling inside the chains trying to unlock

himself with the magic key with fingers slippery with sweat and terror.

It was difficult trying to do it UPSIDE DOWN – he hadn't practised that – and the roars of the hungry Beast below were terribly distracting, not to mention Toothless flapping round the cage getting in the way and squeaking, 'Crisis! C-c-crisis! This is a crisis!'

So all in all, he had only undone HALF of the chains by the time the cage reached the darkness of the tree-cover, which was not part of his plan.

Hiccup had calculated that in order to survive, he would have needed to have undone ALL the chains by this point, so that he would have time to undo the cage door as well.

But life is imperfect, and down, down, down went the cage, as Hiccup desperately cast off another chain and fiddled with the next.

'This is a B-B-BAD BAD plan!' yelled Toothless.

'Too late...' muttered Hiccup, nonetheless heartily agreeing with him. 'Too late...'

'DON'T FORGET ALL DRAGONS HAVE THEIR WEAK SPOTS!' he could hear Camicazi's encouraging voice, above all the rest. 'GO FOR HIS EYES! OR BITE HIM ON THE NOSE! DRAGON NOSES ARE VERY SENSITIVE!'

Oh, very helpful, Camicazi, very helpful... thought Hiccup. *What if he doesn't obligingly hold me up to his nose? What if the only part I get close to is the* TEETH?

'OR PLAY DEAD!' Camicazi shouted. 'I'VE KNOWN THAT TO WORK!'

What if I actually am dead? thought Hiccup.

Down, down, down went the cage... the next lock was tricky and the key stuck for a second... Come on come on come on... Hiccup practically *wept* with frustration as the lock refused to budge...

... *Ping!* The lock flew open, and clang clang clang the chain fell to the cage floor.

Only one more to go...

WHAM!!!!!!

The watchers on the rope bridges jumped back at the suddenness of the explosion of greenery as something like a volcano erupted from below.

The head of the most enormous Beast.

Hiccup saw nothing, just felt the tremendous crazy impact. The cage buckled upwards like crumpling tissue paper as an unimaginable force hit it from below.

'Eeeeek!' squeaked Toothless in terror.

Clang, clang... the last chain went down and Hiccup crawled out of the heap of chains and fitted

the
key
into the
door of the cage
with trembling fingers…

BAMMMMM!!!!

The cage was hit again and
rocked violently to the left. Hiccup
desperately tried to hang on and
turn the key while swinging maniacally
through the air.

He knew what the Beast was doing. He
had seen it so many times before. The creature
was playing with his prey before he ate it, like
a killer whale tosses a seal upon its nose before
consuming it.

CRRUNCHHHHH! Camicazi flinched
as the Beast hit the cage again.

And then there came the ear-splitting siren shriek
of a Beast attacking for the final time.

The jaw-dropping CLANG! of twenty-foot long

fangs crunching on a metal cage.

The jungle swayed violently beneath them in whirlpool waves.

The Beast roared again.

And then there was silence.

The crowd let out a low moan of satisfaction.

Fishlegs muttered, 'Oh... I'm sure he's *fine*... he's *always* fine... in the end... isn't he?'

'THANK YOU GREAT THOR, O KING OF THE JUNGLE AND THE ISLANDS AND EVERYWHERE ELSE!' yelled the mad Chief Berserk. 'BRING UP THE CAGE AGAIN!'

To the great cheers of the watching Berserks, they began to winch up the rope.

Up and up it came, and the cheers got louder as the rope came out of the jungle...

... and all that remained of the cage that had hung on the end of it was one solitary wicker rag hanging mournfully off the hook.

Camicazi stared mesmerised at those straggly

wicker remains, hanging there lopsided and
pathetic.

'Prepare the next Fiancé!' yelled the Chief
Berserk. 'Winch up the cage!'

'What's happened? What's happened?'
moaned Fishlegs, unable to see through
the carpet of Scarers attached to his cage.
'He *hasn't* got out…?' said Fishlegs as they
prepared to attach HIS cage to the winch.

Down Hiccup plunged

17. THE BEAST

Hiccup plunged down from the broken cage…

… and was caught mid-air by the unfeasibly large hand of the Dragon Monster, snatching him out of the ether as Hiccup had seen smaller dragons do with bluebottles. (I am afraid that there is an excellent but rather revolting reason for this. Dragons like to eat their prey alive, a bit like you might prefer a nice juicy plump raspberry to one that has been squashed on the ground.)

and was caught mid-air by the Dragon Monster who threw him into the air again…

The Beast threw Hiccup up into the air again,
and threw back his head to catch him in his jaws.

The mouth opened up like a big black cave,
edged with razor-sharp teeth like stalactites, and
Hiccup just had time, as he somersaulted through the
air, to shout 'HALT!' in Dragonese, before he fell into
the Creature's mouth...

Absolute blackness, and a heat that burned, and Hiccup was just thinking, as well he might, *This really is the end now...*

... when the Monster reached inside his own mouth, and fished Hiccup out by the end of one talon, ju-u-u-ust before he swallowed.

'HALT!' said Hiccup again, coughing wildly as he hung from the Creature's talon, dripping with the disgusting green goo of the dragon's saliva.

The Monster drew Hiccup up to his big yellow eye and took a good look at him.

And in between coughs Hiccup took a good look at the Creature too.

He could not believe what he saw.

It was a *Seadragon*.

And not just any old Seadragon, either.

It was an exceptionally rare Seadragonus Giganticus Maximus.

Hiccup recognised it because he had met one of them before, a year or so ago, on his very first adventure as a Warrior-in-Training.*

What was a *Seadragon* doing here?

The Beast was chained to the ground.

He drew great rasping, asthmatic breaths that were painful to hear, and his skin was worn as dry

---

* Please read Hiccup's first adventure, *How to Train Your Dragon*.

as cracked old parchment. More choking still were the great drifts of smoke that came billowing turgidly out of his nostrils – a pea-soup smoke of stifling, unimaginable, desperate despair.

The forest had grown up around him. A wood of ash had grown up through his spines. His neck was bound not only with metal, but also with rings and rings of choking thorns that were so thick about his face that he could barely move.

Hiccup had never seen the like of the chains that bound that Beast.

It was unimaginable to think of how huge the forge must have been in which those chains were built. For each link was the width of a room in an ordinary house. It would have required maybe fifty men to carry just one. It must have been an almost superhuman task of ingenuity to put those links together, and drive the stake deep enough into the ground so that the great Beast could not work his way free.

The Seadragon's great yellow eye met Hiccup's, and so profound was the maddened melancholy of that eye that Hiccup's first thought was of pity rather than fear, even though the Beast was opening its mouth again, apparently deciding he was a curiosity, but quite safe to eat.

Poor Beast, thought Hiccup. *Poor Beast…*

That moment of pity was what saved Hiccup, for if he had been scared he would have been too frightened to think.

But the pity he was feeling reminded him of the sad story of Hiccup Horrendous Haddock the Second, and at the same time the image of Alvin's Mother popped into his head as she felt the scar on Toothless's chest. *'How strange it is that they have a scar in exactly the same place…'*

Looking down over the Creature's fingertips, Hiccup could get a good view of the Beast's chest.

And on that chest, *right* above the heart, was a fine streak of a paler green…

… the mark of an ancient wound, healed so long ago that there was only the faintest tracing of it on the surface.

Hiccup thought of a dragon, sitting quietly on a beach next to the body of its dead Master. The fresh wound on its chest, still bleeding from the Stormblade, would not kill it. But its heart was broken all the same.

'*Furious!*' Hiccup shouted out.

'*YOU are the Dragon Furious!*'

Now the dragon *really* paused.

It sat, unwinking like a statue, looking back

through the years, and its indifferent eyes become focused and intent.

When at last the dragon spoke, it was in a voice that had not been used for so many years that it creaked and groaned like the Berserks' rattling chains.

'That WAS my name, once,' growled the dragon at last. 'What is my name to *you*, Human? How dare you use it? And how did you know it? And why do you speak in the sacred tongue of the greenbloods?'

Hiccup could barely believe it.

YOU are the Dragon Furious

But this was indeed the Dragon Furious, imprisoned one hundred years ago by Grimbeard's men in this terrible wooded island prison.

'I know your name,' said Hiccup, 'because I am a descendant of your human blood-brother... I AM Hiccup Horrendous Haddock the Third, the son of Stoick the Vast and Valhallarama of the White Arms and Chunky Thighs... and I am a Dragon-whisperer like my ancestor, Hiccup Horrendous Haddock the Second, who was once your blood-brother. By the love you once bore my ancestor, I beg you to hear me. Look, I am speaking to you in Dragonese...'

Hiccup was looking the Beast straight in the eyes, and he quickly closed his own, for that mighty golden gaze was like a laser beam.

'You are speaking the truth,' said the Seadragon in surprise.

Seadragons' eyes can tell such things.

'Much good it may do you...' it said wearily. 'I should warn you, Boy-Who-Has-a-Name-I-Once-Loved, that not a speck of that love remains. Not a jot. Not a whisper. One hundred years of captivity has drained every last drop of that love from me, and I am cured for ever. If I were to have the time again, I would not tarry in that Cursed Bay to weep precious salt tears over his dead body, so that the humans could wrap me about in chains and bury me in this forest. No, I would spread my wings and take off into the bright blue sky and leave him for the fishes to eat... I have been well punished for my weakness in loving and trusting a human.'

Hiccup's heart sank. He had been rather relying on the hope that the Seadragon might have a soft spot for the descendant of his blood-brother.

But he said as confidently as he could (for you have to be assertive with dragons or they do not respect you), 'I have not come here to talk to you about the past, O Mighty One. I am here to set you free.'

'*You?* Set ME free?' drawled the Seadragon sarcastically. 'Look on my chains, human worm... I have been gnawing on these manacles for the past century or so, and still they bind me. How will YOU set ME free?'

'I have the key,' said Hiccup, producing it from his pocket. 'Eat me, and the key is lost to you for ever... Strike a bargain with me, and I can set you free.'

There was a long pause.

What the dragon said next was very, very important. Hiccup did not know HOW important until much, much later.

'I feel it is only fair to warn you,

Boy-Who-Has-a-Name-I-Once-Loved, that the only way I can ever be truly free is if every last human being is dead and sleeping under the soil. The one hope that has stopped me all these years from setting fire to this cursed forest jail, and sending us all to Valhalla in a puff of smoke, is the thought of REVENGE. The thought that one day, I would lead a Dragon Rebellion that finally wiped the humans from this earth for ever. For what the last, failed Rebellion taught me was that humans and dragons cannot share this world. They are irreconcilable enemies. You Have Been Warned, Boy. Release me at your peril.'

'Be c-c-careful,' whispered Toothless to Hiccup. 'Be v-v-very careful...'

But Hiccup was young and optimistic, and hopeful by nature. So he replied, 'Then I will bind you with promises. A dragon cannot break a promise, if he swears on his heart.'

'What is your bargain?' asked the Seadragon.

Toothless crept on to Hiccup's shoulder. His horns were right down, his ears back. 'M-m-make it a good one,' he whispered. 'Tie him up well with his promise. Chain him soundly. Trust Toothless, this dragon is d-d-dangerous...'

'My bargain is,' said Hiccup, 'that I will set you free, in return for your promise that you will help me release every single human being on this island.

And that you will not harm me, or any other human, in the future. That you will fly to the great wildernesses of the north, or to the Great Oceans in the west, where there are no humans to remind you of this terrible time of captivity, and live there in freedom and happiness. Do you promise?'

There was a long silence.

'I promise,' said the dragon, repeating Hiccup's words exactly.

'Cross your heart and hope to die?' said Hiccup.

The dragon made a swift slashing movement across his heart with one talon, and said the words. 'Cross my heart and hope to die...'

So Hiccup set free the Dragon Furious.

Every chain, every manacle, took time to unlock, for Hiccup had to find the tiny keyhole in the giant padlocks that bound the Beast, and the padlocks themselves were so smeary and slippery with a century of moss and fungus that those keyholes were hard to find. And every time he put the key in to an ancient keyhole with shivering fingers, he prayed to Thor that the rust of eons would not make it unworkable. But though the keyholes stuck for a second, and creaked complainingly, yet still they turned, squeaking like rodents and clankingly resistant.

Those Hysterics really were genius inventors.

It was particularly satisfying to Hiccup to release the Beast's wings. When he unlocked the first wing with that tiny click of the lock, it was unrecognisable, entwined with thorns and clogged with brambles. Hiccup watched as the wing shook for a second – and it was as if the forest itself was shaking as it worked its way free of the clinging choke of the greenery and rose up like a great Viking sail, ragged with holes and trailing whole unearthed trees.

Up and up it rose, and Hiccup fought his way almost feverishly over the dragon's back, slashing a path through the undergrowth with his sword, skidding on the slime-dripped scaly surface, in his excitement to get to the other wing and release the dragon entirely.

Up and up rose the wings, and the dragon heaved his great belly up too, tearing trees up by the roots as he staggered to his feet. Hiccup punched the air in joy, and let out a wild whoop as the dragon unfurled himself to his greatest extent and his wings waved wondrously in the wind like impossibly enormous military banners, tattered but triumphant.

18. DYING LIKE A HERO

Meanwhile, back up at the Berserk Treetop Village, Fishlegs was having his own problems.

Alvin had insisted that HE should be the next to go.

'Good luck, Fishlegs!' shouted Humungously Hotshot the Hero, as Fishlegs's cage was winched over the green abyss. 'Remember, you die a HERO, and a Fiancé of Tantrum O'UGerly!'

1st Fiancé: 'YOU BETCHA!'

3rd Fiancé: 'TOO RIGHT...'

9th Fiancé: 'YESSIREE!'

'I die a Hero, I die a Hero,' muttered poor terrified Fishlegs, as the Scarers swarmed six-deep around his cage, shrieking: 'He's go-o-o-oing to di-I-I-I-ieeee... He's go-o-o-oing to di-I-I-I-ieeee...' – 'I die a Hero... oh... *for Thor's sake...*'

'HA HA HA HA HA HA HA!' roared the watching Berserks. 'Look at all those Scarers! He's terrified!'

'Please... just let me die a HERO,' said Fishlegs to himself. 'And not a BIG JOKE...'

To Fishlegs's immense surprise, he heard what he thought was the sound of CAMICAZI's voice shouting

louder than all the rest (which would be typical of
Camicazi, for she had a particularly penetrating pitch
when she wanted to be heard). 'SING!' shouted the
Voice-That-Sounded-Like-Camicazi, 'SING YOUR
TRIBAL ANTHEM!'

And Fishlegs remembered that *Hiccup* had
done just that, when he was about to die on the
slopes of the Volcano.*

But what Tribal Anthem should he sing?
Where was he from? Who knew from whence
Fishlegs's lobster pot had set sail thirteen and
a half years ago?

Again, Fishlegs found out who he was
while sitting in the dark, in a moment of
dreadful peril.

I am a Hooligan, thought Fishlegs, *by
adoption, if not by birth.*

And he began to sing the Hooligan
Tribal Anthem, which he discovered for
the first time was strangely appropriate to
himself:

How to Twist a Dragon's Tale tells this story.

BRAVO! HURRAH!

I didn't mean to come here,
And I didn't mean to STAY;
It's just where the sea wind BLEW ME
ONE ACCIDENTAL DAY,
WHAT A HERO!!

The Scarers lessened around Fishlegs's cage as he was winched above the abyss. They began to fly off as the singing made Fishlegs less scared and therefore less smelly. Seeing this, Fishlegs's voice grew stronger, and he began to shout the words out defiantly, pushing the Scarers away as he yelled out the words.

'It wasn't where I meant to be,
And it wasn't where I had my start,
But now I'll never leave these rain-soaked bogs
Because Berk is where I left my heart!'*

Seeing the Scarers leaving the cage in great grey drifts, gradually the Berserks stopped laughing.

As the cage moved lower down, the last of the Scarers rose up like butterflies, leaving Fishlegs clearly visible, chest out, shouting the words at the top of his voice.

There is nothing the Tribes of the Archipelago admire more than bravery. Even mad-as-a-hatter Tribes like the Berserks can appreciate and respect it.

So a lone Berserk shouted out, 'He IS a Hero!'

And the Berserks and the Fiancés began to cheer, with rapturous applause and appreciative howls as the cage moved inexorably lower, taking Fishlegs to what

---

* *How to Twist a Dragon's Tale* tells you the origin of the Hooligan Tribal Anthem.

everybody thought would be his Doom.

And that was when it happened.

A great shaking below them all.

Massive trees, of a circumference as broad as a house, shivered like grasses in a meadow, sending unsure-footed Berserks raining down, screaming, into the green abyss below.

'What's happening?' screamed Humungous, as the trees heaved and creaked and the whole forest seemed to lurch beneath them in a slow green wave. 'Is it an earthquake?'

'I don't know...' the Fiancé-Before-Last yelled back, taking a strong grip of the bars of his cage.

The jungle trembled to the excruciating sound of trees being torn out by the roots, and then right before their unbelieving eyes, through the green canopy below, there thrust an impossibly large dragon's head, mouth open wide in a magnificent roar. It broke screaming through the canopy as if it were breaking out of its egg.

Another wild and terrible scream, mighty trees crashing down all around it, and the mighty dragon burst out of the forest, blotting out the moon. It began to beat its torn and ragged wings, and the wind sent a hurricane blast through the trees before the Great

Creature launched itself up and into the air.

'For Thor's sake… for Thor's sake…' whispered Fishlegs, shading his eyes as he looked upwards at the great dark cloud of dragon above, 'for Thor's sake…'

And on its back, perched high on the back of the Great Creature, was the first human being to ride the Dragon Furious in one hundred years.

It was Hiccup.

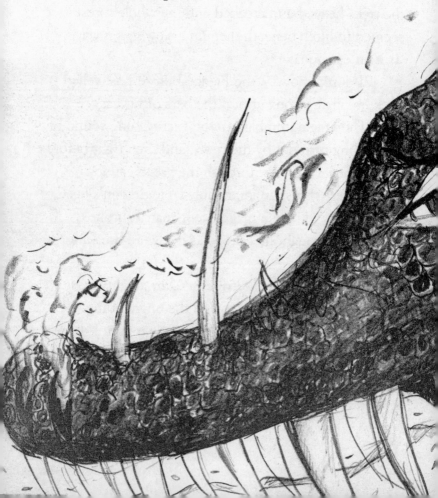

19. AN UNEXPECTED DEVELOPMENT

It was a good moment.

It was a *very* good moment for Hiccup, perched up high on the back of the Dragon Furious, looking down on the Berserks, suddenly turned so small and so weak on their shaking rope bridges.

For their part, the Berserks looked up in awe and absolute astonishment at the mighty dragon hovering above them, the tiny little figure sitting upright on its back.

'HALT!' yelled Hiccup Horrendous Haddock the Third. 'HALT! The Beast of Berserk is now under MY power and control. DO WHAT I SAY or else with one lick of his flames he will turn this whole wood into fire and inferno.'

The Chief Berserk's mouth fell open. 'The Beast...' he whispered. 'I don't believe it... the Beast... how did the boy do it? Is he magic? He must be magic!'

Alvin couldn't believe it either. He had turned as white as his teeth. 'How does he do it?' he muttered. 'How does he do it?"

'RELEASE THE FIANCÉS!' yelled Hiccup

266

Horrendous Haddock the Third. 'WINCH BACK FISHLEGS! RELEASE ALL THE PRISONERS HELD IN THE TREE PRISONS! RELEASE THEM OR THE DRAGON WILL SET FIRE TO THE VILLAGE!'

'How does he know about the tree prisons?' gasped the Chief Berserk. 'WE WILL NEVER SURRENDER!' he yelled, shaking his fist up at Hiccup and the Dragon Furious. 'WE HAVE FIRE-SUITS, YOU KNOW! AND WE ARE NUTTERS!'

'WE CERTAINLY ARE!' yelled the other Berserks on the bridges.

It was fortunate that Camicazi intervened at this point, because Hiccup had no real intention of setting fire to the forest.

But Camicazi had wriggled along her tree branch until she was directly above the Chief. And now she dropped down like a little cat, timing it perfectly so she landed right on top of him.

The Chief wasn't expecting a small blond child to drop unexpectedly out of the night sky and hold a very sharp knife indeed to his throat. He let out a strangled scream.

'Listen here, you plankton-brained, clanking

Howl of a loser!' whispered Camicazi. 'Unless you do exactly as Hiccup says you won't need a Fire-Suit because I will kill you right now, with pleasure, and you can trust the word of a Bog-Burglar on this one...'

The Chief grew thoughtful.

However nutty he was, he was still rather keen on making it through to the morning alive.

'Don't kill him unless you have to, Camicazi!' Hiccup called out.

'Oh, but I may have to,' grinned Camicazi.

Camicazi had been the most difficult prisoner the Chief had ever had. Despite being so small, it had taken five grown Uglithugs to capture her, and she had been so rude when she arrived on the island that she had made one of the Berserks cry.

The Chief had a horrible feeling that she meant exactly what she said.

'Ah... on second thoughts...' said the Chief with an apologetic cough. 'Perhaps you have a point... EVERYBODY DO WHAT THE RED-HAIRED BOY SAYS!'

Now the Berserks may have been nutcases, but like all the Tribes in the Archipelago, they were obedient to their Chief.

So there was pandemonium on the rope bridges as the Berserks galloped, clanking like a load of metallic elephants, to all of the prison cells all across the island. And you had to hand it to the Berserks, once they were given a task, they executed it very faithfully indeed. They had spent the last one hundred or so years guarding these trees. Not a single prisoner had managed to get out in that entire time. Every Berserk would happily have laid down his life to prevent an escape.

And now they went about releasing the very same prisoners with the same mad keenness and energetic efficiency. If a prisoner was too weak to climb the rope that was let down into the tree, the Berserks actually descended the rope themselves, and brought the prisoner up in a fireman's lift on their massive shoulders. Some of the poor prisoners had been in there so long, they had forgotten what life outside was like, and they did not want to leave.

But they were given short shrift.

'EVERYBODY OUT!' yelled a massive Berserk, shouldering a poor shrinking old man who had forgotten his name, and what Tribe he was, and did not want to leave the tree frogs who had been his friends for the past sixty years. 'BOSS'S ORDERS! YOU'RE ALL TO LEAVE ON THE DOUBLE!'

So before long the rope bridges were packed with lines of confused shuffling prisoners in rags, some with renewed hope in their eyes, others scared and apprehensive, all blinking in the unaccustomed daylight.

'UNLOCK THEM!' yelled Hiccup, as the Dragon Furious hovered above the scene of chaos, 'UNLOCK THEM AND SET THEM FREE! The dragons as well!'

So even the Chickenpoxer and the Windwalker were unlocked from their chains by the eager Berserks.

'Do you want to know how old I am, you iron-clad ignoramus?' smiled Camicazi, still holding her knife to the Chief's throat.

'Not particularly,' said the Chief of Berserk.

'I am eleven and a quarter,' grinned Camicazi. 'And even though I am of course the toughest and most brilliant eleven-year-old in the Archipelago, how good does that make you feel, a great big Let's-Go-Crazy Warrior like you, to be beaten in battle by a titchy-witchy little eleven-year-old?'

Not very good, actually. The Chief of Berserk felt a little like crying himself.

And once the Fiancés and the prisoners were set free of course, they grabbed any weapon they could find and a pitched battle ensued between Fiancés and Berserks, a battle that is known in the Sagas as The Battle of the Treetop Madmen. The Berserks going crazy is an incredible, awesome sight. They swung

through the trees, brandishing their swords
and cutlasses and snorting and roaring like wild
animals. Some even foamed at the mouth.

The Fiancés had a whale of a time, for they were
all very fine swordsmen.

1st Fiancé: 'TAKE THAT YOU HAIRY
JANGLING BUFFOON! TAKE THAT AND THAT
AND THAT!'

2nd Fiancé: 'Oh, I say, that's a fine Deluxe Lange
you have there, old boy… you must teach me the trick
of it…'

1st Fiancé: 'Oh, no problem, it's just a dexterous
flick of the wrist and—'

Hummungously Hotshot swinging into act!

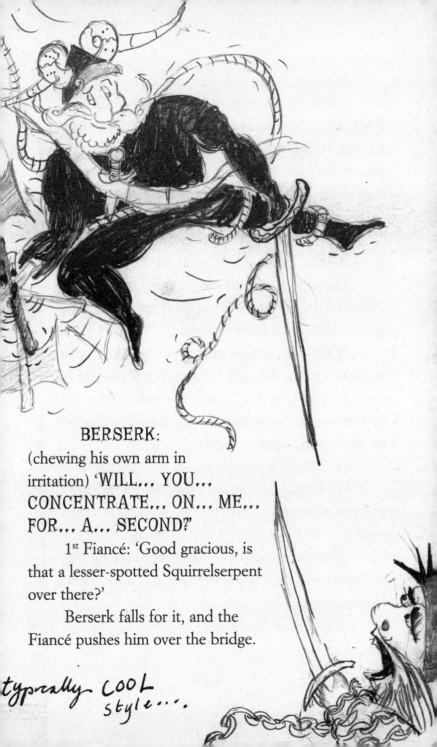

BERSERK: (chewing his own arm in irritation) 'WILL... YOU... CONCENTRATE... ON... ME... FOR... A... SECOND?'

1st Fiancé: 'Good gracious, is that a lesser-spotted Squirrelserpent over there?'

Berserk falls for it, and the Fiancé pushes him over the bridge.

typically COOL style...

Sometimes the old ones are the best.

Camicazi alone managed to dispatch three Berserks – a fine total if you consider the awesome fighting skills of these extraordinary Warriors. (But of course she had the advantage of dropping down on them from ABOVE which gives the element of painful surprise.)

'That'll teach you to try and trim the wings of a BOG-BURGLAR!' yelled Camicazi with relish.

Humongous, of course, fought like a FlashMaster, taking on Berserks three or four at a time, and beating them in style.

When Hiccup saw prisoners from the tree prisons walking into the Berserk Village, free at last, he let out a yell of pure glee. He couldn't believe it. Not only had he defied death himself, but it looked like he had saved the whole lot of them.

He should have known not to rejoice too soon.

He should have known that the moment of greatest triumph can also be the moment of greatest peril.

Hearing Hiccup's cry of relief at seeing the prisoners set free, the Dragon Furious gave a shrug of bitter malice.

And then he threw back his head and sent a great

burst of flame shooting straight at the forest in direct defiance of their agreement.

The whoop of joy died on Hiccup's lips.

The flame hit a particularly large tree, which exploded on impact.

Exploding fire... Hiccup had never seen that before...

'*What about your promise?*' shrieked Hiccup, as the dragon made a lazy revolution in the air, and swooped downwards for another attack. '*NO FIRE TILL YOU LEAVE THE ARCHIPELAGO, YOU PROMISED!*'

As if in answer, the dragon shot out another downward rocket of flame, and another tree exploded, and the fire spread quickly to the very next tree, which went up like a candle, and the drenching sparks that shot upwards into the night sky were like the burning remains of the dragon's worthless promise.

'T-t-toothless *told* you not to trust him,' said Toothless helpfully.

'You promised...' whispered Hiccup, 'you promised...'

'You have to have a heart to make a promise,' growled the dragon. 'And *my* heart was broken long ago. With the half that's left, I'll keep HALF

275

my word. For one year I will stay away from the Archipelago. One whole year, is all I'll give you, Boy-Who-Has-a-Name-I-Once-Loved... and then after that I will return, and I will make you a new promise...'

Hiccup was sure he wasn't going to like the new promise, and he was right.

'The new promise is, I will return, and THIS TIME the Dragon Rebellion will be successful. We shall scourge this world with fire, and leave no wretched human being alive, not a single one. For over the last hundred years I have been looking into the past and into the future, and I tell you this, Boy... humans and dragons cannot live together...'

The dragon's words, dark, terrible words, hissed out above the roaring of the wind around Hiccup's ears.

'NO!' shouted Hiccup. 'That's not true! Hiccup Horrendous Haddock the Second did not believe that and nor do I!'

'Hiccup Horrendous Haddock the Second is DEAD,' said the dragon, soaring higher and higher. 'Look down, Boy, look down at the REAL world.'

Hiccup looked down at the little sprinkling of green islands in a blue sea below him.

'In this world,' continued the dragon bitterly, 'my

dragon-brothers are everywhere in chains. Humans are enslaving us like dogs... they are riding us like horses... they are removing our fire and clipping our wings and breaking our hearts.

'There is no longer room on our planet for dragon and human,' said the dragon, and now he just sounded infinitely weary. 'And when I look into the future, I see we are running out of time. I also see that if I do not stop you, YOU, YOU Hiccup, will be the end of us all... YOU will send us into our final oblivion...'

'Who *me*?' squeaked Hiccup. 'But I LOVE dragons! You've got this all wrong!'

'If you grow to manhood, that will spell the end of us,' repeated the dragon. 'And so I will call the dragons from far and wide, from the depths of the ocean and the ends of the earth, and we shall fight the final battle before it is too late.'

'NO!' yelled Hiccup. 'NO, NO, NO, NO, NO!'

At the top of his swoop, the Dragon Furious tipped over into a barrel roll.

Down, down, down, Hiccup fell from the dragon's back.

And then the Dragon Furious spread wide his ragged wings and flew off towards the frozen north.

Down, down, down Hiccup plunged, shrieking,

'NO! NO! NO! NO! NO!'

He barely knew what he was saying 'NO!' *to*,
whether it was no to the idea that humans and dragons
could not live together, or no to Fate, or just no to
gravity itself, which was taking him
inexorably downwards.

20.

THIS REALLY HAD BEEN A VERY BAD NIGHT...

Meanwhile, as the trees burned before them and around them, Camicazi stopped teasing Berserks.

'FIRE!' she yelled. 'FIRE!!!'

'MAKE FOR THE HARBOUR!!!!' bellowed the Chief Berserk.

Prisoners, Berserks, Fiancés – all stampeded down the rope bridges away from the direction of the fire, towards the direction of the Berserk Harbour.

And above them, down, down Hiccup plunged, with Toothless shooting after him.

Down, down, the boy fell from the heights of the Dragon Furious, and he *would* have plunged to his death if the Windwalker hadn't shot towards the falling boy.

Dragons are magnificent flyers. They have evolved to catch their prey mid-air, and so the Windwalker timed it perfectly, shooting upwards in four great gliding flaps of his wings, catching Hiccup by the back of his collar as he fell through the air.

Well, he timed it *nearly* perfectly.

He caught Hiccup slightly off-balance, and the weight of the boy sent him into an aerial spin, and boy and dragon carried on plunging down into the inferno below, bouncing off a tree branch, and landing, by pure fluke, on one of the rope bridges, which shivered and whined, and threatened to break... and held.

Hiccup was thrown unconscious, and the Windwalker had entangled one of his wings in the ropes of the bridge.

Squeaking wildly in alarm, Toothless landed on his Master's chest, and licked his face frantically to wake him up. The entire Forest was in flames now, and trees that had taken hundreds of years to grow were turned in an instant from wood into bonfire.

Hiccup's eyes opened. He staggered groggily to his feet.

'I... er... need help...' stammered the Windwalker, and Hiccup tugged at the tangles that were holding the Windwalker's wing. He had nearly worked it free, and in the nick of time too, for BOTH ends of the rope bridge were now in flames, when a limping figure appeared at the end of the bridge.

It is never wise to forget about Alvin.

You should always be aware of him, plotting in the shadows, creeping up behind you, cloak flapping behind him like a malevolent bat. As indeed he was creeping up behind Hiccup right at that very moment,

I shall GET YOU Hiccup Horrendous Haddock the Third, even if it is the LAST THING I ever do.

tiptoeing so carefully on the rope bridge that his ivory foot barely made a tap, Stormblade fixed in his metal attachment, furious grin on what remained of his face.

You would have thought that Alvin would have used the pandemonium to quietly escape *himself*. After all, Alvin was as much a prisoner as the poor souls hidden in the tree trunks. He had spent nearly a whole year cooking for the Berserk army, partly in chains himself, forced to be subservient and polite. He was certainly not allowed to *leave*. So why did Alvin not take advantage of the chaos to slip away to

freedom?
Why was he
not, like the
others, fleeing
the fire?

The answer
is that over the
years, Alvin's hatred
of Hiccup had been
growing in his brain like
some quiet cancerous weed
that sprouts its tentacle shoots
into every nook and cranny. Now it
had grown so poisonously, mazily, *dizzily*
strong that it had taken over his brain entirely,
choking the life out of every other thought. Even his
sense of self-preservation – which used to be Alvin's
strongest point – was now weaker than his hatred of
Hiccup.

(Do not feel too smug, readers. Alvin is not
the first, nor shall he be the *last* human being to be
so consumed with hatred that he would rather die
HIMSELF than see his enemy live to fight another
day.)

Up behind Hiccup, Alvin crept, and Toothless

only just had time to
shout, 'Behind you! Behind
you!' for Hiccup to turn, and
draw, and meet Alvin's sword, blade
on blade.

The two swords clashed with a bright clean
ring: Grimbeard's Best and Second-Best Swords, the
Stormblade and the Endeavour, and the boy and the
man began to fight.

This was
their third
swordfight, but
never had there
been such desperate
circumstances as the bridge
burning at both ends in the remains
of what was once the Woods That Howled.

Alvin thrust and swore, and lunged at the
boy, and between every parry Hiccup called out to the
Windwalker, was he all right, and could he get free?

Even burnt and tired, Hiccup's sword-fighting
had improved, and he was winning the fight, and Alvin
was swiping increasingly desperate hooks at him, when
one of the ropes of the rope bridge burnt through, and
the bridge plunged suddenly downwards, knocking
Hiccup off-balance so that he fell through the ropes,
and with one flailing hand ju-u-ust caught the bridge,
so he was hanging over the blazing inferno with
one… hand… alone.

Smiling a bitter smile of triumph, Alvin approached.

'I've got you now, Hiccup Horrendous Haddock the Third,' triumphed Alvin the Treacherous, and the old villain held his hook into the burning, flaming ropes of the bridge until it was smoking hot. And then he raised his hook to bring it down on Hiccup's hand.

'ALLLVI-I-I-I-INNNNN!' came a wild, weird screechy shout from the smoke behind. And then again 'ALVVI-I-I-I-NNNN!'

And the hook paused, allowing Hiccup to put his other hand up on the bridge, and then his elbow.

If Hiccup could have seen it, that old villain, Alvin the Treacherous, had turned as deathly white as if he had seen a ghost.

And if Hiccup hadn't been so busy ha-a-a-auling himself up by his elbows and back on to the bridge, he would have seen also an extraordinary figure, riding towards them through the smoke.

It was Alvin's Mother, riding on the Chickenpoxer.

21. A BIG SURPRISE FOR ALVIN

If it hadn't been such a perilous moment, it might have been funny.

It was such a bizarre sight.

Twenty years without light had sucked all the colour out of the witch and she was white as bone all over. Her brilliant shock of chalk-dry hair blew five feet long behind her. Her faded eyes were still half-blind, but her other senses were so acute now that she could make her way around like a bat using radar.

The Chickenpoxer was bucking madly, trying to get her off, but the witch was made of stern stuff, much sterner than Fishlegs, and she held firm, and rode him at the figures on the bridge.

Alvin had now turned a ghastly green.

Who can blame him?

He hadn't seen his mother in twenty years.

And she was pretty scary.

'Mother???' whispered Alvin the Treacherous querulously. 'Is it *you*, Mother?'

'Help him up, you FOOL!!' raged the old lady, wheeling around in the air above their heads on the Chickenpoxer. She didn't seem terribly pleased to see

her son, considering they had been parted for such a long time.

'What's happened to you?' she scolded, taking in his missing leg, eye, hair, nose and arm. 'Look at the *state* of you! I leave you with ve-ry clear instructions on how to become the King of the Wilderwest, and you can't even hang on to your own *limbs*! Don't you see, you meddling MORON, you can't let that little rat fall into the fire, he's got the SWORD!'

From a splendid, dreadful villain on the brink of a great and evil triumph, Alvin turned in one split-second into a small boy caught in the act of doing something stupid.

'No, *I've* got the sword...' said Alvin, holding up the Stormblade rather pathetically, as if it would impress her.

'IDIOT!!!' screamed Alvin's Mother, bringing the Chickenpoxer to a screeching halt above their heads. 'It's the OTHER SWORD! Help him up, help him up! And take the sword off him!'

Alvin turned back to Hiccup, hissing, 'I can't believe it... you set her free... this is the worst thing you've ever done to me...'

But it was too late.

Hiccup had already hauled HIMSELF up by his

elbows, and the Windwalker had worked his wing free, and Hiccup now scrambled up on to his back and the Windwalker sprang into the air…

… and the bridge burnt out at both ends, and fell into the abyss.

Alvin screamed, and Alvin's Mother leant down from the Chickenpoxer and grabbed him by the hook as the bridge fell down from under him.

But as the witch grabbed the hook she let out a horrible shriek.

For Alvin had held the hook in the flames of the bridge only a few moments earlier. And that had turned the hook burning, scorching, *frying* hot.

'Aaaaaieeeeeeeeeeeeeeee!' screamed Alvin's Mother. 'AAAAIEEEEEEE!'

The touching reunion between mother and son lasted precisely one minute.

There was a horrible, sulphurous smell of burning flesh, and Alvin's Mother let go of the hook.

DOWN Alvin plunged, into the Inferno.

And in one blink of an eye he was gone.

The witch did not hesitate.

She leapt from the Chickenpoxer's back and down into the fire herself.

I don't know what she was hoping to do.

But the flames swallowed *her* too, in one greedy gulp. And I *would* have said surely even Alvin and his Mother could not have escaped this time, from an entire burning Forest?

But I won't because I have been wrong before.

22. THE CHILDREN ARE FOUND

Stoick the Vast hadn't slept much the previous night, for he was worrying about his son Hiccup, who had not come home.

At first light, a search party set out, and quickly found Fishlegs's note, and so they were already halfway to Berserk when they saw the island was on fire.

'FIRE! FIRE! BERSERK IS ON FIRE!'

By the time the Hooligan search party reached the island, most of the Berserks had already escaped, in ships headed who knows where?

Some prisoners were still trapped at the very tops of the trees, and had taken off shirts or trousers, and were waving them above their heads to make themselves visible to their rescuers.

Soon the scene was one of shouting chaos, with the rescuers trying to spot the trapped Vikings through the smoke, and shouting orders to one another – 'I've found one here!' or 'There's two more down in that tree there!' – before flying down to safety.

'What an EXCELLENT bonfire,' smiled Snotface Snotlout, when he arrived at the scene of the conflagration. 'I suppose it's too much to hope that the Useless was in the middle of it, and burnt himself down to a little Useless crisp?'

It *was* too much for Snotlout to hope for.

To Stoick's intense relief, right at the back of the beach was a semi-circle of Fiancés, blackened and weary, and in the middle of the semi-circle were Fishlegs, Camicazi, Hiccup and Humungously Hotshot the Hero.

'Humungous!' bellowed Stoick, for once deeply relieved to see the irritatingly perfect Hero. 'You saved my son's life AGAIN!'

'*No*,' said Humungous, putting his hand on Hiccup's shoulder. 'This time, he saved *mine*...'

'*And* we completed the Impossible Task!' said Fishlegs, proudly opening his lobster pot and pointing to five full pots of honey inside.

'*And* I've found eleven other people who actually WANT to marry Princess Tantrum,' said Hiccup, pointing at the Fiancés.

Fishlegs looked at his lobster pot full of honey.

And then he gave the lobster pot to Humungously Hotshot.

'Are you sure?' said Humungous.

'Yes,' said Fishlegs. 'The Fiancé-Before-the-

Fiancé-Before-Last was who she really loved.'

The other Fiancés found that their love for Tantrum O'UGerly had rather dwindled after their experiences on the island of Berserk.

So in *their* case, it can't have been True Love, after all.

1st Fiancé: 'And we will stand beside you,

Humungous, when you go to claim your bride! I feel like a bit of a set-to with that UG the UGerly!'

'Ooh,' Camicazi said, swishing her sword. 'Me too! Yippee, I can't WAIT to spill some Uglithug blood.'

'No way,' said Stoick firmly. 'I am taking *you* back to your mother.'

'Whose Chief do you think you are?' howled Camicazi in disappointment.

But Stoick would not give way. Looking for Camicazi was what got them in this mess in the first place and he wasn't going to take the risk of her getting lost again.

'Don't worry, we will rescue your Stormfly for you,' said Humungous. 'Word of a Hero.'

'You may need this,' said Hiccup.

And he fished around his pocket, and took something out, and gave it to Humungous.

It was a key.

The key that opens all locks.
that Toothless swallowed in Hysteria

23. HOW UG THE UGLITHUG FINALLY LOST HIS DAUGHTER

The Sagas tell how the very next day Humungously Hotshot, dressed all in black, sailed up the Gorge of the Thunderbolt of Thor, and into the heartland of UG's territories, right under the nose of the sleeping Screechdragons, and somehow escaping the notice of the swooping Raptortongues.

That impudent Hero, Humungously Hotshot, stole into UG's castle at dead of night. Nobody knew how he got in, for UG's castle was supposedly impregnable. There were no fewer than TWENTY locked doors before you even began to get in to the Inner Castle.

But somehow Humungously Hotshot got through them all and went tiptoeing through the castle, somehow he located UG's bedroom (probably from the snoring) and *somehow* he entered the heavily-guarded room without awaking the sleeping sentries. And ever so gently, ever so quietly, he left four pots of honey made from the bees of Berserk by UG's bedside.

The fifth pot he poured carefully into UG's favourite pair of slippers. And when UG awoke the next morning, his daughter was gone.

The window was wide open, the curtains flapped in the wind, the bed was empty.

The bird had flown.

There were some other items of value missing.

A very rare golden Mood-dragon that UG had been keeping in a cage in his Dragon Stables until it learnt better manners and didn't run away from its true Master. For some reason it seemed to think that it belonged to that wretched little Bog-Burglar child who had stolen it in the first place.

And a huge, heavy Throne that UG had only recently transported all the way from his Western Beaches, with some difficulty, and was about to start the process of re-decorating with the crest of the Uglithugs.

That was where the other ten Fiancés had come in handy, lifting the Throne.

UG the Uglithug's ships sailed towards the Archipelago, searching for the runaways and the missing valuables.

But the boat belonging to Humungously Hotshot the Hero, *The Peregrine Falcon*, is the fastest boat in the Archipelago.

And swifter than eagles and faster than fireflies that boat had sailed, down the misty Gorge, and away.

A day or so after *that*, Stoick the Vast was left a present on his beach.

The present was an unusually handsome one.

Bigleg the Slowtop found it when he went out early to go fishing, and he rushed back up to sound the bells to wake up the Village.

Half asleep, the Hooligans and the Bog-Burglars – who had stayed with the Hooligans to sleep off the effects of a rather splendid feast to welcome Camicazi home – staggered down to the Harbour.

And there, sitting on the beach as if it had been there for ever, was a huge and handsome THRONE of almost god-like proportions.

At the feet of the Throne was a lobster pot, and

in it was curled a gorgeous sleeping Mood-dragon, the colour of a bright golden coin. Around her neck was a letter.

'Stormfly!' cried Camicazi joyously, rushing forward to greet the beautiful dragon, who yawned luxuriously, and awoke. 'Are you all right? Are you hurt?'

'I bit that rude Uglithug,' smiled the Mood-dragon, speaking in beautiful Norse. 'Many,

many times…'

'Oh you clever, clever girl!' said Camicazi, gathering the Mood-dragon in her arms.

The Hooligans and the Bog-Burglars gathered around the Throne to admire it. They had never seen such a Throne in all their lives.

'I knew it was one of ours, after all,' said Stoick the Vast, pointing to the Hooligan coat of arms on the back. 'But I wonder where it came from?'

'Don't sit on it!!!!' said Hiccup urgently. 'There's something very wrong with this Throne, and nobody should sit on it.'

'A Throne isn't very useful if you can't *sit* on it! What do *you* think we should do with it, Old Wrinkly?' Stoick asked the Elder of the Tribe, Hiccup's grandfather, an ancient old man with skin as dry and wrinkly as an old piece of driftwood.

'A Throne found on a Haunted Beach,' said Old Wrinkly, 'may not be a good Omen. And I agree with Hiccup… I have a bad feeling about this Throne. But something also tells me that we should not destroy it.' Old Wrinkly thought a while. 'You should put the Throne in the Harbour. It won't do it any harm to be underwater again. Then nobody can sit on it and bring a Curse on themselves… but we know where it is… in case we need it someday.'

'Let's leave it here for now and we'll put it in the Harbour tomorrow,' decided Stoick. 'NOW, there is something so much more important to think about. Breakfast!'

'Oh *goodee*!' bellowed Bertha, clapping her hands together. 'Double helpings of roast beef and Great White Shark fins for me!'

'The letter is addressed to you, Hiccup,' said Stoick, handing it to his son, and ruffling his hair affectionately. 'Never mind, son,' he added awkwardly, clumsily aware that this might be a disappointing moment for Hiccup, and he ought to say something. 'You were a little young to be getting married, you know. Better luck next time, eh?'

'But Father, I never WANTED to get married, it was like this...'

It was all FAR too complicated for Stoick's brain, which was a little underpowered at the best of times, let alone before he'd had his morning coffee, and so Hiccup gave up trying to explain. Stoick had already stomped off up the beach anyway.

Camicazi and Fishlegs crowded round him as he opened the letter.

Out fell a piece of paper, and a key.

Dear Hikkup, Fishleggs and Kamikazi,

We are off on our hunnymoon and we just stopped by to return these. Thank you for all you have dun for us, and for the loan of this key, which came in very useful. The ~~Feiws~~ Fiancés sent there best wishes.

Yours Truely,
Humungously Hotshott
and
Tantrum O'Ugerly Hotshot
(HEROES for HIRE)

BY DRAGON MAIL

To Hikkup, Fishleggs
and Kamikazi,
(Fellow Heroes)
Isle of Berk
BARBARIK AR

Valentine.

Yours sincerly,

?

Dear Fishlegs,
Thankyou for the Bog-Rose,
I wore it for my wedding.
Love Tantrum P.S. nice poetry!
Have you ever thought of becoming a BARD?

The letter was written on the back of Fishlegs's poem to Tantrum.

'T-t-toothless's key!' said Toothless joyfully. 'Can Toothless keep it?'

'You certainly can, Toothless,' said Hiccup, tying it round Toothless's neck. 'I have to admit, if you hadn't eaten that spoon, all would have been lost. You saved the day again, Toothless, you saved the day again... but no more eating inedible objects, eh?'

Toothless shook his head earnestly, and then stuck out his chest as if the key were a medal and rattled it carelessly at Stormfly.

'Ooh, Toothless,' cooed Stormfly, 'you're so official and important...'

'Listen,' said Camicazi, pointing out to sea, 'I think that's Humungous and Tantrum singing...'

If the three of them screwed up their eyes they could just see the black fin-like sail of *The Peregrine Falcon*. There were angry storm-clouds brewing above, and the waves were beginning to rise up with the ominous white tops that signalled an approaching gale, and rain was starting to fall.

But both the voices that they could hear faintly singing above the whistling wind were wildly cheerful.

First Humungous, a completely tone-deaf,

out-of-control voice that slid up and down the scales with no regard for any actual *tune*:

> '*Once I loved Truly, and my Heart paid the price,*
> *Now let me love Truly, Thor, let me love TWICE!'*

And then another, female voice, the voice of Tantrum O'UGerly, singing an old Viking Archipelago song called *Not the Settling Kind*. It went like this:

> '*I have never cared for castles or a crown that grips too tight,*
> *Let the night sky be my starry roof, and the moon my only light,*
> *My Heart was born a Hero, my storm-bound sword won't rest,*
> *I left the Harbour long ago on a Never-ending Quest,*
> *I am off to the horizon where the wild wind blows the foam,*
> *Come get lost with me, Love, and the sea shall be our Home…'*

And then Humungous again:

'*My one True Love vanished, and my heart broke
that day,
But once you've loved Truly, Thor, then you know
the way*!'

Was it Hiccup's imagination, or was the female singer's
voice just as bad at singing as the male voice? Surely
that wasn't possible.

'I shall never love again,' sighed Fishlegs, putting
the poem in his pocket.

'Well, people do say that being crossed in love
is very good for poets,' said Hiccup. 'And look at
Humungously Hotshot. It worked out all right in the
end for *him*. *You* may get a second chance, too,' said
Hiccup. 'After all, you *are* only thirteen.'

The three friends and the two little dragons
began to wander down the beach towards the steep
windy cliff path that led back up to Hooligan Village.
Hiccup absent-mindedly threw a stone over his
shoulder and up the beach.

The stone landed a little distance away from
the Throne, hunched quietly on the sand. The waves
were beginning to lap at the Throne's feet, and for
a moment, Hiccup fancied there really was a giant
invisible ghost sitting there, fruitlessly commanding

the waves to be still, to go back, just as Grimbeard the Ghastly had wanted to turn back time, all those long, long years ago.

But of course no human could rewind the past, or stop the tide from coming in.

Hiccup remembered the promise of the Dragon Furious, a dreadful promise indeed if it were to come true:

'I will return, and THIS TIME the Dragon Rebellion will be successful. We shall scourge this world with fire, and leave no wretched human being alive, not one single one.'

The dragon's heart had been broken long, long ago in a tragedy too terrible for Hiccup to comprehend. A tragedy like that had ghastly consequences. Ghosts were launched who haunted beaches in the Archipelago to this very day… Hearts like this dragon's heart hardened, and twisted into dark and hungry forests.

But Hiccup was young and optimistic.

Human hearts could break and heal and beat again… Maybe *dragon hearts* were the same.

Far in the distance, he thought he could hear Humungous still singing:

And so I said
to that chained
up maniac, THAT'LL
teach you to lock
up a Bog-
Burglar...

'Once I loved Truly, Thor, and my heart paid the price,
Let me love Truly, Thor, let me love TWICE! '

Surely it will be all right in the end, thought Hiccup.

When the dragon said: 'Unless I stop you, YOU, YOU, Hiccup, will be the end of us dragons... YOUR choice will send us into our final oblivion...'

Why, *that* couldn't be true, could it? Hiccup *loved* dragons. Some of Hiccup's *best friends* were dragons.

'C-c-c-ome ON! ' Toothless swooped down impatiently, and dug his claws into Hiccup's waistcoat, and tried to drag him more quickly up the cliff path. 'We're going to m-m-miss all the breakfast! And Toothless thinks it might be eggs and bacon!'

Hiccup shook off his dark thoughts and turned away from the Throne.

His father was right. He would think about it tomorrow.

There might be storm-clouds to the *south*, where Humungous and Tantrum were headed into the future, and storm-clouds to the *west*, over the island of Tomorrow, where this tragedy happened in the past.

But *right now*, *right here*, a bright morning sun was shining over Berk, and everybody was safe, and breakfast was on the table.

Toothless landed on Hiccup's shoulders, and Hiccup hurried after his two friends. Eggs and bacon were *Hiccup's* favourite too, and Tomorrow...

... well, Tomorrow could wait, for Thor's sake.

EPILOGUE

Was it *really* sixty-five years ago that I discovered my destiny in the darkness of Berserk?

It is another world, a vanished world, the dragons, the witches, the storms, the swordfights and the shipwrecks of my childhood.

The boy I was is so far away to me now.

Sometimes I dream that same dream, though, the one that haunted me long ago, of the ghost-lady, and the ship, and the boy on his dragon. The ghost of course is the ghost of Hiccup the Second's mother, Chinhilda, and she haunts the Bay of the Broken Heart, calling out for the baby who was taken from her by her own husband.

That same dream still shakes my old body awake sixty-five years later in an ague of shivers and trembling in the dark watches of the night.

But the dream has slightly changed.

When I dream that dream now, *I* am the ghost-lady, calling out to my lost child.

'*Hiccup!*' I cry longingly, '*Hiccup! Come back to me, Hiccup...*'

And I hold out my arms.

But the boy on the dragon is disappearing into

the clouds, fading into the airy glory of the next world, and there is absolutely *nothing* I can do to stop that from happening.

The boy turns his head.

I cannot see his face at this distance, but he is heart-breakingly young.

I hear his voice, very, very faintly.

'*Don't worry!*' he calls. '*I will come back, I promise…*'

And here he is.

CAN THE HOOK
SURVIVE THE FLAMES?

CAN *the Seadragon Furious organise a second Dragon Rebellion that aims to extinguish the entire human race? And if so, which side is Toothless going to be on?*

WHAT is the terrible choice that Hiccup is going to have to make?

And WHEN *is everybody going to find out that he has the Slavemark?*

And, last but not least, SURELY, SURELY, *that one-legged, one-armed, no-nosed, follically-challenged villain* **Alvin the Treacherous** *has not survived, yet again, the fire that burnt down the island of Berserk, and lived to fight another day????*

Watch out for the next volume of Hiccup's memoirs,
How to Steal a Dragon's Sword

This is Cressida, age 9, writing on the island.

Cressida Cowell grew up in London and
on a small, uninhabited island off the west
coast of Scotland where she spent her time
writing stories, fishing for things to eat,
and exploring the island looking for dragons.
She was convinced that there were dragons
living on the island, and has been
fascinated by them ever since.

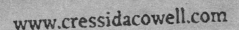

www.cressidacowell.com

HOWDEEDOODEETHERE!

For your latest news on all things dragon
and Cressida Cowell please follow:

 @cressidacowellauthor

 @cressidacowell

 facebook.com/
cressidacowellauthor

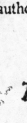

 Toodleoon for now...

LOOK OUT FOR
CRESSIDA COWELL'S
NEW SERIES

The
Wizards
of
ONCE

Once there
was Magic...

This is the story of a young boy Wizard, and a
young girl Warrior, who have been taught to
hate each other like poison.

#wizardsofonce